Have you got all the *Chestnut Hill* books?

Lauren Brooke

Chestnut Hill

A Chance to Shine

SCHOLASTIC

With special thanks to Catherine Hapka

First published in the UK in 2009 by Scholastic Children's Books
An imprint of Scholastic Ltd
Euston House, 24 Eversholt Street
London, NW1 1DB, UK
Registered office: Westfield Road, Southam, Warwickshire, CV47 0RA
SCHOLASTIC and associated logos are trademarks
and or registered trademarks of Scholastic Inc.

Series created by Working Partners

This edition published by Scholastic Ltd, 2013

Text copyright © Working Partners, 2009

Cover photography © Equiscot Photography

The right of Lauren Brooke to be identified as the
author of this work has been asserted by her.

ISBN 978 1407 13660 8

A CIP catalogue record for this book is available
from the British Library

Printed and bound by CPI Group (UK) Ltd, Croydon, CR0 4YY
Papers used by Scholastic Children's Books are made from
wood grown in sustainable forests.

1 3 5 7 9 10 8 6 4 2

www.scholastic.co.uk/zone

"Well? What do you think?"

Honey Harper turned from examining a cute beaded belt to see Josh Hartley grinning at her. He had grabbed an Atlanta Braves baseball cap from a rack in the department store's well-stocked accessories section and pulled it on over his wavy blond hair.

"Smashing," Honey pronounced.

"That's what I told him," Honey's friend and roommate Lani Hernandez agreed, looking up from pawing through a table holding more baseball caps. The three of them were at the mall as part of a group outing that included Honey's other two best friends, Dylan Walsh and Malory O'Neil, as well as Malory's boyfriend, Caleb Smith, and Honey's twin brother, Sam.

"You did not," Josh corrected Lani. "You said, and I quote, 'Whoa, awesome!' Somehow 'smashing' sounds much better."

Dylan wandered towards them with Malory at her heels. "That's just you getting all hot and bothered over Honey's sexy British accent," Dylan teased Josh.

"Oi, cheerio, but she's got you there, mate!" Caleb called out in a cartoonish accent.

Honey rolled her eyes. "That's the worst Cockney accent I've ever heard!" she chided. She hoped the others hadn't noticed her blushing furiously. Josh was what Dylan liked to call Honey's semi-boyfriend. The two of them had liked each other for a while and enjoyed hanging out together as often as they could. Unfortunately, that wasn't as often as either might have liked. Honey was an eighth-grader at Chestnut Hill Academy along with the other three girls, while Josh, Caleb and Sam all attended nearby Saint Christopher's School, a boys' school better known as St Kit's. Both boarding schools kept their students busy – in addition to their rigorous academic studies, there were plenty of other activities, from horseback riding and other sports to regular charity projects and various extra-curriculars and special events.

Those special events included school dances, and Honey and Josh had been to a couple of those and shared some sweet, romantic moments together. Even so, Honey still felt a bit awkward about referring to herself and Josh as a couple, at least in public. She preferred to take things slowly and figure out exactly how they felt about each other at their own pace.

Her friends mostly respected that, though Dylan and Lani couldn't resist teasing her sometimes when the whole group met up in the small town of Cheney Falls, located just a couple of miles from both campuses. These occasional Saturday-afternoon outings were usually raucous and fun, whether the group spent their time at the mall or wandering along the town's quaint shop-lined streets.

"Rats," Lani muttered, digging through the baseball caps. "Looks like they don't have any Colorado Rockies hats left."

"Maybe they never had any," Josh pointed out. "Why bother to stock stuff from such a lame team?"

Lani shot him a look. "Them's fighting words, dude," she warned playfully. "You'd better make sure we never play ball together. I've got a mean slider pitch that could take a guy out, if you know what I mean."

"Better be careful, Lani," Honey put in. "If you hit him with the ball, it means something called a walk, doesn't it?"

Josh looked impressed. "That's right," he said. "The batter would get to go to first base."

"Since when did you start paying so much attention to baseball, Honey?" Malory asked in surprise, pushing back a strand of her curly dark hair.

Lani laughed. "Yeah, last time I noticed, Honey didn't know a walk from a bunt. Or baseball from football, for that matter."

"I try not to pay any attention at all to baseball myself, of course." Dylan wrinkled her nose. "But they do have a point, Honey. Since when are you a fan?"

"I don't know." Honey couldn't help being mildly surprised herself. When she and her family had moved to the United States less than two years earlier, she'd barely heard of the all-American sport. "I suppose I must've absorbed something during all those long, dull conversations Lani and Sam are always having about it." She shot a fond look at her brother, who had been fascinated with baseball from the moment they'd arrived in the US. He and Lani had bonded over that as well as the fun sense of humour they shared. These days they were a pretty tight couple, though – like Honey and Josh, or Malory and Caleb – they didn't get to spend nearly enough time together.

Sam didn't appear to notice Honey's glance. He was hurrying towards them from another part of the accessories area. "Check it out," he told Lani, skidding to a stop in front of her. "I just found a Rockies cap on the display rack up front." He twirled in place, showing off the hat he was wearing.

"Ooh, gimme! I want that!" Lani grabbed at the hat. Her father was a commander in the US Air Force and as a result of his job, the family had lived all over the country. However, they'd been in Colorado for the past five years, long enough for Lani to consider it home.

"Sorry, finders keepers," Sam teased, dancing just out of reach.

Honey smiled as she watched them. It was great to see her brother looking so lively. Soon after moving to the US, he'd been diagnosed with leukemia for the second time in his life. Things had been touch and go for a long, difficult while, but he'd finally come through his treatments and started to recover. He was now in full remission from his symptoms, though his doctors had explained that he wouldn't be considered officially in remission from the disease until he'd been cancer-free for five years. Still, they were optimistic enough about his current condition to say that he could return to school, and so he'd started at St Kit's at the beginning of the spring term. He wasn't able to stay there as a boarder like most of the other boys, but the family home was close enough for him to commute to the school as a day student.

All in all, it had been a tough couple of years for Honey and her family. *But that's all over now*, she thought. She sighed contentedly, sneaking a peek at Josh, who had taken off the Braves cap and was looking through the rest. *And it was worth the wait. Because now everything is pretty much perfect.*

"OK, enough baseball." Dylan tossed aside the Mets cap she'd just tried on, then fluffed her red hair. "Like I said, I'm not exactly a fan, and besides, none of these are working with my outfit." Her eyes brightened when she spotted another rack nearby, this one crammed with cowboy hats in all shapes and sizes. "Ooh, but rodeo style, on the other hand. . ."

She rushed over and started trying on the cowboy hats. Honey joined her. "You know, this reminds me of England," she remarked, casting a look at her brother as she picked up a cute red felt cowboy hat.

Dylan looked confused. "Huh? Cowboy hats remind you of England?" she said. "I thought we invented the cowboy right here in the good old US of A."

Instead of answering, Honey just grinned, stuck the hat on her head, and burst into a song from the musical *Annie Get Your Gun*.

"Whoa!" Lani exclaimed, hurrying over from the

baseball display. "Where'd *that* come from? Honey, you've got a really awesome voice!"

"Thanks." Honey felt a little sheepish when she noticed several adult shoppers nearby glancing her way in surprise. She didn't usually set out to make herself the centre of attention, but seeing the cowboy hats really had brought back memories. "That song is from a musical I was in at my old school in England."

"*Annie Get Your Gun*?" Dylan raised her eyebrows. "I saw an off-Broadway revival with my parents a couple of years ago. Did you really have a part in that?"

"She did," Sam said. "Honey was brilliant. Stole the show."

Once again Honey felt herself blushing. "It wasn't a big deal at all," she protested. "Just a silly school production – a bit of fun."

"Don't let her fool you." Sam grinned. "Honey may act the shy one, but truth is, she's a show-off at heart. She used to force the whole family to sit down in the living room and watch her perform these long, long plays she'd written herself. She even swiped Mum's best tablecloth to use as a stage curtain."

"Really?" Lani raised a sceptical eyebrow at Sam. "If anything, I'd have thought that sounded more like something *you'd* do."

The others all nodded. Honey could sometimes be reserved and quiet in new situations, while Sam was outgoing, fearless, and relentlessly talkative.

"Why are you guys acting so surprised?" Malory spoke up. "We already knew Honey could sing."

6

Dylan blinked at her. "We did?"

Malory nodded. "Don't you remember? When she first started riding Minnie, she'd sometimes sing to her when she thought nobody was listening."

"You're right," Honey admitted. "Before I came to Chestnut Hill I hadn't ridden that many different horses, even though I had my own pony back home. So I'm often a bit anxious when I ride one that's new to me. Singing helps settle my nerves."

"I know." Malory smiled at her. "I do the same thing sometimes when Tybalt's having an especially tense day. Singing helps us both get through it."

Honey smiled back, though she knew Malory was being kind by comparing their two situations. It was no secret that Malory was one of the best riders at Chestnut Hill. That was why she was the captain of the junior jumping team, the competition team for seventh and eighth graders. Ali Carmichael, the school's young, talented director of riding – who also happened to be Dylan's aunt – had awarded Malory the post based on her skills as well as her empathy with all the members of her team, human and equine alike. Honey hadn't made the jumping team, but she didn't mind. She was having a wonderful time improving her riding with the help of Moonlight Minuet, better known as Minnie. The beautiful, gentle grey mare belonged to Dylan's parents, who had leased her to Honey.

"I guess Minnie doesn't realize how lucky she is," Dylan commented, grabbing another hat off the rack.

"All this time she's been getting private concerts from our own secret superstar, Honey Harper."

"Maybe she can come over to St Kit's sometime and sing to Gent," Caleb said, referring to his own handsome grey gelding, which he rode for the St Kit's jumping team. "He's been giving me some trouble with counter canter lately."

"Hey, get in line," Lani protested, giving him a playful shove. "If she's going to sing to anyone, it's Colorado. The last time I asked him for a lead change, he almost bucked me off." She grinned, showing that she really didn't mind the spunky buckskin gelding's antics. In fact, Honey was pretty sure that Colorado's attitude was the main reason he and Lani got on so well. "Anyway, I feel stupid, now, Honey," Lani added. "I'm your roommate, and I had no idea you could sing like that."

"Join the club," Dylan said. "But now that we know, we should see about getting her an audition for the next season of *American Idol*."

"No way!" Honey felt alarmed at the idea of trying out for the popular television show.

"No chance," Sam put in. "She's not American, remember?"

"She lives here," Dylan retorted. "That's American enough for TV."

"Yeah." Josh tapped the brim of Honey's hat with his fingers, smiling down at her. "That cowboy hat really suits you. Maybe you guys should consider doing a production of *Annie Get Your Gun* for your next Chestnut Hill fundraising event."

Honey quickly pulled off the hat, half wishing she'd never put it on. On the one hand, she did love singing and performing. Somehow, being on stage made her forget to be self-conscious. She was able to throw herself into a song or speech as if she were another person. She'd been too busy to think much about that since coming to Chestnut Hill, but thinking about it now she realized she missed it.

But it was also disconcerting to be the centre of attention when she *wasn't* performing. Especially when Josh started looking at her like that, and she wasn't sure how to react. . .

Lani seemed to sense her discomfort. "Hey, enough with the hats," she said, grabbing the cowboy hat out of Honey's hands and tossing it back with the others. "Who's up for a milkshake? I could really go for a double strawberry at the Dairy Den." She waved a hand in the direction of the rest of the mall.

"Ooh, sounds good," Honey agreed, relieved to have the spotlight taken off her. "But no strawberry for me. I'm dying to try their new Hershey's Kiss flavour milkshake!"

"There's a Hershey's Kiss flavour? OK, that settles it," Dylan joked, linking one arm through Honey's and steering her towards the food court. "First baseball, now Hershey's Kisses? I'm thinking assimilation is complete. Honey's a true American girl now!"

2

"Do we have time to stop in and check our emails?" Lani asked as she and Honey hurried down the main path through Chestnut Hill's sprawling campus. It was Monday afternoon, and they'd just finished their last academic class of the day. There was a break before their regular riding lesson down at the barn, meant to give them enough time to return to their dorms to change into their riding clothes. However, their algebra test had run over, making Honey and Lani a few minutes late.

Honey checked her watch and nodded. "I think so, if we hurry," she said, turning down the side path leading to the student centre. "Plus I want to check on my eBay account. I'm bidding on that signed baseball cap for Sam, remember?"

Lani grinned. "Oh, right," she said. "Guess you're not the only one who's assimilated to American life, huh?"

"Not a chance. Even spending so much of his time in the hospital, Sam settled in quicker than I did!" It felt good to joke about her brother that way. There had been a time when Honey had feared Sam might never leave that hospital again. Knowing that her beloved twin was just a few miles away, healthy and active again, attending his own classes and messing around with his own friends, made her feel warm and happy inside.

Soon she and Lani were seated beside each other at the row of computers provided for the students' use. Honey signed into her online account, planning to log straight in to the auction site in case she ran out of time. But when her email inbox popped up, she noticed that one of the messages was from Josh, and couldn't resist clicking on it. When the message opened, she laughed out loud.

"What is it?" Lani asked, glancing over.

"See for yourself." Honey turned the monitor to make it easier for her friend to see. Filling the screen was a full-colour image of the original film poster for *Annie Get Your Gun*, with Honey's face Photoshopped on to it atop the heroine's body.

Lani laughed, too. "Sweet!" she exclaimed. "Josh is pretty handy with Photoshop, huh?"

"I know. I'm going to print it out so I can show Dylan and Mal later." Honey hit a couple of keys to make that happen, then glanced over at Lani again. "Anything interesting in your inbox?"

"Nothing like that." Lani shot a look towards the colour printer, which had started humming in preparation for printing out the image. "Just an email from Guadeloupe catching me up with all the family news."

Honey nodded. Lani had four older sisters, so there was always a *lot* of family news!

By the time the two of them logged off a few minutes later, Honey and Lani had to run to Adams House to change and then sprint down to the stables so they wouldn't be late. When they arrived at the main barn, they almost crashed into Dylan and Malory, who were standing in the entrance peering down the aisle.

"What's going on?" Lani panted. "Are we late?"

"Huh? Oh, I don't know." Dylan shot them a quick, uninterested glance. "What I want to know is, where are the horses?"

Blinking, Honey looked past her friends into the tidy, clean-swept barn aisle. Inside, she saw the other members of their intermediate riding class, including Lynsey Harrison, Dylan's room-mate. Honey also spotted Kelly, one of Chestnut Hill's two full-time stable hands, coming out of the tack room at the far end of the aisle carrying a couple of dirty saddle pads. What she *didn't* see was the familiar sight of a dozen or so horses and ponies hanging their heads out over the half-doors of their stalls. In fact, the barn appeared to be completely unoccupied by equines.

"Yo, Kel, where are our ponies?" Dylan called out as the stable hand came closer. "If Ms Carmichael really wants us to slog out into the pastures and catch them ourselves, I hope she doesn't expect us to be ready on time."

Lani poked her on the shoulder. "Don't be silly, Walsh. You know Ms Carmichael *always* expects us to be ready on time." She glanced at Kelly. "But yeah, what's the deal?"

Kelly just winked at them. "You'll find out soon enough."

At that moment another familiar figure came into view at the end of the aisle. This time it was Aiden Phillips, the energetic and enthusiastic young jumping coach.

"There you are, girls!" she called out, hurrying towards them. "Ready to get started?"

"What do you think?" Lynsey crossed her arms over her chest and tossed back her long, sleek blonde hair. "Do you see any horses standing here with us? Duh."

Ignoring Lynsey's obnoxious comment, Ms Phillips stopped and surveyed them all with a smile. "You won't be needing your riding helmets today," she said, gesturing towards the GPA hat dangling by its chin strap from Dylan's arm. "Or your ponies, either. Just your dancing shoes, though paddock boots will do."

"Huh?" Malory glanced down at her well-worn boots. "Dancing shoes? What do you mean?"

"Oh, and we won't be working in any of the rings today," Ms Phillips added. "You can't dance on sand, after all. Come with me."

She hurried out the doorway behind them before anyone could respond. Honey turned and stared after her.

"What's going on here?" Dylan murmured.

Lani shrugged. "Maybe it's some kind of fitness training," she suggested. "Ms Carmichael spent, like, half our last lesson complaining that we all had legs like limp noodles."

Honey giggled at the image. Ms Carmichael had said no such thing, though she *had* made a comment or two about the importance of staying fit to ride.

"Are you kidding?" Lynsey let out a snort. "I come to this school to ride. If I need fitness training, I'll call my mother's personal trainer for tips."

"Come on." Dylan was already hurrying after Ms Phillips. "Let's go see what's up."

They caught up to the jumping coach halfway between the main barn and the secondary stable block in a flat, grassy area where the girls sometimes hand-grazed their ponies. "All right," Ms Phillips called out as they straggled towards her. "Please form two lines across the yard."

The girls obeyed. Honey found herself standing in the back row between Lani and Jennifer Quinn, a petite dark-haired seventh-grader from Granville dorm who normally rode a school pony named Flight. Malory was on Lani's other side. Dylan ended up in the front row along with Lynsey, Paris McKenzie of Curie dorm, and the final member of their current class, seventh-grader Abigail Loach of Meyer.

"OK, Ms Phillips," Dylan spoke up. "Now are you ever planning to tell us exactly what we're doing today?"

The coach grinned. "As a matter of fact, I am – right now," she said. "You see, we're starting a new module today – dressage to music!"

Honey exchanged an interested look with Lani and Malory. She'd seen the musical kurs ridden at the Olympics and other high-level competitions. Some of the performances were completely magical, making it seem like the horses were actually dancing to the music.

"Wow, musical dressage?" Malory whispered, her eyes sparkling with interest. "I've always wanted to try that!"

"Me too," Honey replied.

Lani nodded. "Sounds a lot more fun than the regular dressage boot camp with Mr M."

Honey grinned. Roger Musgrave came in once a week to coach the riders in dressage. He was an ex-military man who was strict and tough, running his lessons like an army drill. It was impossible to imagine Mr Musgrave clicking on a stereo and inviting the ponies to dance!

Only Lynsey looked less than enthusiastic. "Dressage to music?" she said, pronouncing the words with the same tone and expression she might use to say *steaming pile of dog poo*. "Why?"

"How about because it's fun?" Dylan retorted.

"Fun, yes." Ms Phillips nodded. "But that's not all. This is a brand-new module that's just been introduced to the Virginia riding curriculum. Chestnut Hill will be the first school to try it out."

"Cool!" Lani said. "So when do we start?"

"Right now." Ms Phillips turned and gestured to someone who'd just stepped into view from the direction of the stable block. Honey saw a tiny, slender woman dressed in tights and legwarmers hurry over to join the coach. "I'd like you to meet Ms Nadine Savier," Ms Phillips continued. "Nadine is—"

"A ballet dancer!" Honey blurted out, too surprised to hold her tongue.

15

"That's right." Ms Phillips smiled. "So you've heard of her?"

"Of course!" Honey said. "I took ballet lessons for a while back in England. Everyone there knows Ms Savier. She's a famous prima ballerina from the Royal Ballet in London."

"Call me Nadine, *chérie*, please," the ballerina said in a rich, kind voice with a strong French accent. "And you are too kind."

Lynsey still looked less than impressed. "So are you a rider, too, or what?" she asked Nadine.

"Oh, I'm afraid not." Nadine smiled. "Though I would love to learn someday."

"Ms Carmichael and I decided that before you girls learn to dance on your horses, you should learn how to dance on your own two feet," Ms Phillips explained. "That's why Nadine is here."

"Yes, I hope to share with you all the magic of dance," Nadine said, stepping forward gracefully and offering them a little bow. "Besides which, dancing is wonderful exercise for fitness. Shall we begin with some stretching exercises?"

At first Honey couldn't help feeling self-conscious as she sat on the ground touching her toes and stretching into the air. Who ever heard of exercising or dancing while dressed in breeches and paddock boots? But as the lesson went on, she gradually forgot about how absurd she might look. Nadine made everything seem fun, and before long Honey was really enjoying herself. She could tell most of the others were, too. Malory was graceful and athletic and caught on quickly to everything they were asked to do. Dylan was somewhat less graceful, though she managed to make up for that – mostly, at least – with enthusiasm and a good sense of rhythm. Lani was probably the most athletic of all of them, but she couldn't quite get the hang of the intricate footwork. More often than not she ended up facing a different way from everyone else, though she usually ended up making a joke about it at her own expense and reducing her classmates to laughter.

"Please be serious," Nadine said sternly as Lani cracked everyone up for about the tenth time after tripping over her own foot. "How can you expect to learn to dance if you are always making jokes, *chérie*?"

"I don't know," Lani puffed, shaking out her left ankle as she climbed to her feet. "But I'm starting to think this is hopeless. I have two left feet!"

Nadine bent down and peered at Lani's feet, which were encased in the battered cowboy boots she often wore for riding lessons. "No, I am afraid you are quite mistaken," the dancer pronounced seriously. "You most certainly have a right foot as well."

That made everyone laugh again, including Lani. Honey heard a snort from the sidelines and looked over to see that Ms Carmichael and Mr Musgrave had come out of the barn to watch. The riding director was laughing along with everyone else, while the stern dressage coach was rolling his eyes, one corner of his mouth twitching. Meanwhile Nadine winked at Lani and offered her a brief smile before demonstrating the next exercise.

Once they'd finished the warm-up and learned some basics, Nadine taught them a short dance routine, which they performed to some classical music that she'd brought along on her portable CD player. As she followed the moves, Honey felt her body relaxing into the dance. Even though she hadn't taken a ballet class since she was ten years old, when she'd quit to focus her free time on her pony, Rocky, she felt some of the once-familiar positions coming back to her. *This is fun!* she thought. *Although it feels somewhat different performing in riding boots.*

"No, no, Lani!" Nadine called out just then, interrupting Honey's thoughts. "You are off the beat. Please, try to feel the music!"

"Is that better?" Lani yelped, hopping around in what appeared to be a random fashion. "Am I on the beat now?"

"Maybe she's just not feeling the whole symphony thing," Dylan suggested. "It might help if you threw on some hip hop or something with more drums."

Nadine pursed her lips. "I think not," she said. "I ask you, would you perform a jazz routine to a funeral march? No more should we try to perform ballet to hip hop! The dance is all about the mood of the music."

"Sorry." Lani sighed. "Guess my arms and legs are just in a bad mood today."

Nadine's stern expression relaxed into a smile. "All right, fair enough," she said. "Shall we all try it again from the top?"

In the end, the whole class successfully danced the

entire routine, prancing around the yard more or less in time to the music. Even Lani mostly stayed with the others, though she had to add a few extra skip-steps to catch up now and then. When they finished, huffing and puffing from the exertion, Ms Carmichael, Ms Phillips and Mr Musgrave applauded.

"Brava!" Ms Carmichael called out.

"Thank you so much, Nadine," said Ms Phillips. "I know we've all learned a lot today." She turned to the class. "Now, I want you girls to remember everything you've learned today about feeling the music and the mood, because you'll be able to use that when you get back on your horses."

"Cool!" Dylan said, while Malory nodded with interest.

"I'll try," Lani put in with a grin.

"Me too," Lynsey said. "But I'm sure it would be a lot easier if I were riding Blue."

Honey shot her a sympathetic look. Lynsey had brought her own pony to school with her. Bluegrass was a well-trained, impeccably-bred show pony who had carried Lynsey to first place at shows all up and down the east coast. However, he'd recently suffered a stall injury and would be out of commission for another few weeks at least.

After Ms Phillips dismissed the class, Honey reached out and touched Lynsey on the arm. "I know how you feel," she told her. "I'd be gutted if I couldn't ride Minnie for such a long time as you're off Blue. But at least you have Quest to ride – you've done so well with him so far, I'm sure you'll get through this, too."

"Of course we will," Lynsey said with a little frown. "If I can take him over a showjumping course with no faults, I certainly hope I can manage a few dressage moves. But I'd still rather be riding Blue."

Dylan rolled her eyes. "Just to make sure we remember Quest is *vastly inferior* to Blue," she said as Lynsey left the yard. Glancing at her friends, she added, "Come on, all that dancing made me hungry. Last one to the dining hall's a rotten egg!"

3

"Happy birthday!" Honey shouted in unison with Malory and Lani as all three of them leaped into Dylan's bedroom.

It was early Wednesday morning and the room was dim, with only two girl-sized lumps visible beneath the covers on the twin beds. As Honey and the others began singing an enthusiastic version of "Happy Birthday to You," both lumps started to stir.

A second later Dylan sat bolt upright, grinning from ear to ear. "Thanks, guys!" she said when her friends finished the song. "I can't believe you remembered!"

"Are you kidding, Walsh?" Lani joked. "You only reminded us every five seconds for the past two weeks."

Meanwhile the lump in the other bed had turned into a cranky-looking Lynsey. "Do you mind?" she croaked, sweeping off her lavender-scented eye mask. "Some people are trying to sleep here."

"Well, some other people are trying to celebrate," Lani informed her. "Come on, Mal. Bring over the cake."

"Cake?" Dylan's eyes brightened further. "You brought cake?"

"I hope it's not stale," Malory said apologetically as she set a box on Dylan's bedside table. "We bought it Saturday in town – we've had to keep it hidden in Mrs Herson's fridge since then."

"Naturally, she kept telling us we should have asked her to help us bake one from scratch." Honey couldn't help smiling at the memory of their housemother's horror at the store-bought cake. "But when we reminded her that part of the goal was to keep you from figuring out what we were up to, even she couldn't argue with that."

Lani carefully lifted the cake out of the box. A plastic skewbald pony was standing on top, fetlock-deep in icing.

"Oh my gosh! There's a horse on it!" Dylan cried, clapping her hands with delight.

"We got that on Saturday, too." Malory grinned. "See? It looks like Morello."

"You guys are so awesome!" Dylan exclaimed. "I can't believe you did all this, and I never even suspected a thing. Totally sneaky!"

"We learned from the best," Lani said, trading a high five with her. "Dylan Walsh, the queen of scheming."

"Ew, don't tell me you're actually going to eat that?" Lynsey was staring over from her bed, her slim, aristocratic nose wrinkled with distaste. "Didn't you just say it's been sitting around since Saturday? That's, like, four days!"

"Wow," Lani quipped. "Someone's been paying attention in math class!"

"I've also been paying attention in health class," Lynsey retorted. "And gee, I must've missed the part of our nutrition lessons that mentioned cake as a healthy breakfast food."

Dylan shrugged as she swooped one finger through the icing. "It's my birthday," she said, licking it off. "Nutrition and stuff doesn't count on birthdays."

Malory pulled out a cake knife and started passing out slices. Honey sneaked a peek at the other bed. Considering how Dylan felt about her snooty, supercilious room-mate, she could only imagine that the disgusted expression on Lynsey's face was the icing on the cake, so to speak.

"Are you sure I have to do this?" Dylan moaned. "Mme Dubois is probably going to expel me when she sees me in this hat."

Honey stifled a laugh. Dylan did look rather ridiculous dressed in her neat blue and grey school uniform topped off with a crazy striped Dr Seuss-inspired hat.

"Don't be silly," she said, giving Dylan a gentle shove in the direction of their French classroom. "And you know the rules. You can't turn down a birthday dare."

"I'm not so sure about that," Dylan argued. "I'm pleading ignorance. I'd never even heard of birthday dares before you came along, Honey. It's clearly some crazy British custom we Americans shouldn't tolerate, like tea taxes or that extra letter *u* you guys put in words sometimes."

"You can't plead ignorance," Malory said. "You didn't seem to have any problem with this particular custom on *my* birthday when you dared me to eat one of Tybalt's horse treats, remember?"

"That's different." Dylan shrugged. "You like experiencing everything about horses and stuff. People didn't blink an eye when you did that." She reached up and touched the hat. "On the other hand, I have a certain fashion image to protect."

Lani snorted. "Uh oh. You'd better be careful, or you're going to start sounding like Lynsey."

"Oh, no!" Dylan's eyes rounded. She put the back of one hand to her forehead. "If I'm sounding like the snob queen, it probably means I'm coming down with a fever or something. I'd better go to the school nurse and lie down. Tell Mme Dubois I'll be back tomorrow."

"Turning chicken in your old age, Walsh?" Lani grabbed Dylan by the arm. "Come on. I can't wait to see the look on Dubois's face when she sees you. I wonder how you say 'Get that ridiculous thing off your head or get out of my classroom' in French?"

"I don't know," Malory said. "But I have a feeling we're about to find out."

Honey laughed. There had been so many strange new customs, holidays and slang phrases to get used to when she'd first come to America that it was fun to turn the tables on her friends once in a while. None of them had heard about birthday dares before the first time she'd mentioned it, but the dares had quickly become a favourite custom among the four of them. Every time one of them celebrated a birthday, the others put their heads together and came up with dares to be performed in each class of the day. So far Dylan had been forced to speak in Pig Latin throughout English class, to taste at least one bite of every single food on the cafeteria line during lunch, and to work the phrase "beef cobbler" into conversation with Dr Duffy in science class. And there were still several more classes to come. Honey was particularly looking forward to seeing what Ms Carmichael would say when Dylan showed up for their regular afternoon riding lesson with all four of Morello's hooves painted with purple glitter.

"Let's go, Dylan," Malory added after a glance at her watch. "Wearing a goofy hat is one thing, but you know Dubois will flip if we're late."

Dylan squared her shoulders. "OK, OK," she said. "I suppose I'm old enough to handle it. *Allons-y!*"

"Good girl!" Honey leaned forward to pat Minnie as a reward for the crisp, square halt she'd just performed along the centre line of the indoor riding ring. It was cloudy and threatening rain, so their regular afternoon lesson was being held inside. As part of their musical dressage unit, Ali Carmichael had them working hard on some of the basic moves in preparation for adding music later.

"Very nice, Honey," Ms Carmichael called from the centre of the ring. "Lani, try to make sure Colorado doesn't take that extra step after your halt – you'd lose points for that in a test, musical or otherwise. And

Dylan, in case it's slipped your mind, a halt involves a cessation of all motion, not just sort of slowing down and wriggling around for a while."

Dylan let out a groan. "Sorry," she said. "Morello doesn't understand that it's my birthday and he's supposed to take it easy on me!"

"I must have missed that memo as well." Ms Carmichael maintained a straight face, though Honey thought she detected a twinkle in her eye. "Now quit your stirrups, everyone. Let's work on improving your seats."

"Thanks a lot," Lynsey told Dylan as she kicked her custom-made Vogels out of her stirrups and crossed the leathers over Quest's withers. "Why don't you keep mouthing off? Maybe she'll make us ride bareback. That's all I need while being forced to ride this bouncy thing." She shot a disdainful glance down at Quest, who was standing quietly in the line-up.

Honey bit her lip. She'd thought Lynsey had actually started to enjoy her substitute partner lately, but it seemed not. On the one hand, Honey could understand why Lynsey missed her own pony. But she also felt like reminding Lynsey – again – that Quest was an awfully nice horse in his own right. Besides that, she doubted Ms Carmichael was having them quit their stirrups as punishment for Dylan's remark. If the riding director hadn't reacted to Morello's glittery hoof polish when Dylan had ridden him into the ring earlier, a mild complaint wasn't likely to bother her either.

Honey held her tongue, knowing it wouldn't do any

good to mention any of that to Lynsey. Instead, she turned her attention back to Minnie. "Ready to go, girl?" she murmured, giving the gentle grey mare another pat after she'd crossed over her stirrups.

"All right, everyone ready?" Ms Carmichael called, surveying the line of riders. "Good. We're going to do some work on transitions. In dressage, one of your goals should be to have invisible aids. I should see the horse do what it's supposed to do – with you looking as if you're doing virtually nothing except sitting there. Now I want you to pick up a sitting trot, track left at the end of the ring, and then do a shoulder-in down the long side. When you reach the corner. . ."

Honey listened carefully to the rest of Ms Carmichael's instructions. Some of her classmates were looking alarmed, but Honey knew she and Minnie could handle the exercise. Minnie was only an average jumper, but she was outstanding at dressage. When Ms Carmichael called for them to start, Honey closed her legs, asking Minnie to trot. The mare stepped off neatly, rounding her back so that it was as easy for Honey to sit her trot without stirrups as with.

By the time they finished the exercise and halted again, Honey was breathing hard. It was a lot of work to sit there and look as if she was doing nothing! But when she glanced over at Ms Carmichael, the instructor looked pleased.

"Very nice for a first try, everyone," Ms Carmichael said. "Lynsey, I can see that you and Quest are pretty well in tune with each other, but remember to keep your leg on in downward transitions so he doesn't fall on his forehand. Malory, I know Tybalt still has trouble with overbending on the lateral work, but I could see that you were working on it, so just keep trying." She went on to mention a few things to each of the others, then turned to Honey. "That was nearly perfect. Your transitions were clean and crisp, showing that you and Minnie were in perfect harmony. Very nicely done!"

Honey smiled, feeling herself glow with pleasure. Ms Carmichael was an encouraging, positive teacher, but she didn't hand out compliments willy-nilly. If she said they'd done well, she meant it.

"Thanks, girl," Honey whispered, scratching Minnie on the withers. "You really make me look good. I couldn't do it without you!"

"Let me guess." Nat Carmichael grinned and glanced down at his cousin's feet. "You guys must've had a riding lesson right before you came to meet us."

Honey looked down at Dylan's feet, too, and laughed. "Uh oh," she said. "Dylan, you forgot to change out of your paddock boots!"

Malory looked perplexed. "How did you manage to do that?" she asked. "I mean, you had to take off your breeches and put on those jeans, right?"

"What can I say?" Dylan grinned. "I'm very talented."

"Come on, girls," Malory's father spoke up. "We had better get in line for tickets. The movie starts in ten minutes."

28

Honey followed the rest of the group towards the box office outside the Cheney Falls movie theatre. Normally Dylan's parents came to Chestnut Hill to take her out to dinner on her birthday, but this year they were travelling overseas. They'd promised a rain check as soon as they could, but in the meantime Ms Carmichael and her son Nat, a sophomore at St Kit's, had arranged a special outing to help Dylan celebrate. With the help of Malory's father, they were treating the birthday girl and her three best friends to a special weeknight trip to Cheney Falls, complete with dinner and a movie. Honey had been looking forward to it all week.

Soon all seven of them were sitting in the darkened theatre munching popcorn and watching the latest James Bond film. It began with an exciting action scene featuring some impressive equestrian stunts.

"Wow," Lani whispered from her seat beside Honey. "Is that how everyone rides over there in England?"

Honey laughed softly. "Not quite," she whispered back. "At least not anyone I know – thank goodness!"

Dylan heard them whispering and leaned over from Lani's other side. "Hey," she hissed. "Think I could teach Morello to do that last stunt?"

"You mean galloping alongside a train so you can leap off his back on to one of the carriages?" Lani shook her head. "Doubtful, Walsh. Highly doubtful."

Dylan shrugged. "I bet we could do it if I bribed him with enough carrots. Too bad there are no trains running through campus."

"Yeah." Lani rolled her eyes. "Too bad."

Stifling a giggle, Honey reached for more popcorn. Then she leaned back in her seat and turned her attention back to the action on screen.

After the movie ended, they wandered out into the evening air. "That was awesome!" Dylan exclaimed. "Makes me want to become an international spy." She spun around and pretended to brandish a weapon just like Bond.

"International, huh? You'll have to figure out how to pass French class first," Lani commented.

Honey laughed, glancing over at Malory to get her reaction. But Malory didn't seem to be paying attention. She was staring straight ahead. Following her gaze, Honey saw that Malory's father and Dylan's aunt were walking a little way ahead of them. Mr O'Neil had just reached over to take Ali Carmichael's hand in his own.

Now Honey understood why Malory seemed distracted. Ms Carmichael and Mr O'Neil had been dating for just over a month. They'd kept their new relationship a secret from Malory at first, and while she'd forgiven them for that, she still hadn't quite forgotten. Honey suspected it couldn't be easy for her friend to watch her father being romantic with someone else, even several years after Malory's mother had died.

Just then Malory looked over and caught Honey staring at her. Malory smiled, but there was a glimmer of sadness in her eyes. Honey reached over and grabbed her hand, squeezing it without saying a word.

Malory squeezed back. Now her smile looked a little

less forced. "Thanks for being there," she whispered to Honey, too softly for anyone else to hear.

"Always," Honey promised, feeling her heart swell with happiness. With friends like this, and horses like Minnie to ride, and a school like Chestnut Hill, could life possibly get any better?

4

"Ms Hernandez!" Dr Duffy called out as the bell rang and his students jumped up and poured out of science class. "Could you stay behind for a moment, please?"

"Sure," Lani said. She glanced at Honey, Malory, and Dylan. "Go ahead without me. I'll catch up."

"It's OK," Malory said. "We'll wait. We've only got lunch next, and there's always a line by the time we get there anyway."

Dylan nodded. "Besides, I heard there's cooked cabbage today. I'm in no hurry to experience that smell!"

Lani laughed and ducked back into the classroom. The others leaned against the wall outside and waited while the rest of their classmates hurried off.

"I hope she's not in trouble," Malory said. "I told her it was a bad idea to suggest we use yesterday's mystery meat as our next dissection project."

"Nah." Dylan shook her head. "I mean, if this were French or history or practically any other class we were talking about, I could believe Lani was in trouble. But science? Dr Duffy loves Lani. She's his own pet science whizz."

Honey nodded. "I suppose you're right."

Fortunately they didn't have long to wait. Lani burst out of the room just a few minutes later, grinning from ear to ear. "Guess what?" she cried, grabbing Honey and spinning her around in a circle.

"What?" Honey asked, laughing breathlessly. Whatever Dr Duffy had wanted to talk to her friend about, she guessed it was good news.

"My science project won first prize!" Lani exclaimed.

"Shut up!" Dylan shouted, punching her on the arm. "You mean that thing you did about baseball or whatever?"

Lani nodded, still grinning. "It was about baseball trajectories, to be specific," she said. "Dr Duffy just got the call this morning. It won first place in the state science fair!"

"Wow, Hernandez, that's huge! Like, *epic* huge!" Dylan was so excited that she started jumping up and down.

Malory laughed and did the same. "Congratulations, Lani!" she said. "We always knew you were a genius. This just proves it."

Honey and Lani were jumping up and down by now, too. All four of them were laughing and hugging one another. "Thanks, guys," Lani said breathlessly. "But I'll need all you fashion geniuses to help me pick out something to wear to the award ceremony."

Dylan stopped jumping, immediately all business. "Got it," she said. "How much time do we have?"

"The ceremony's Friday night," Lani said. "It's going to be a dressy kind of thing, I guess – like, a fancy dinner and then a lecture from some TV star or something. Dr Duffy is going to be driving me and a guest of my choice up to Richmond or somewhere for it."

Honey smiled, guessing who that guest would be. *I hope Sam doesn't already have any big plans*, she thought. *Because if he does, he'll have to cancel them. He definitely won't want to miss helping Lani celebrate such an important moment.*

Meanwhile, Dylan looked horrified. "Friday?" she said. "But that's tomorrow! That means no time for shopping – we'll just have to make do with what we can scrounge up around the dorm. Hmm, I wonder if Rosie would let you borrow that gorgeous Tadashi dress she wore to the last dorm party? You guys are around the same size. And then there's the issue of shoes. . ."

Now Lani was looking mildly alarmed. "Hold the phone, Dyl. It's a science geek ceremony, not the Oscars."

"Never mind." Dylan looped one arm through hers and steered her towards the door. "We can discuss it over lunch."

"Ready, everyone?" Ms Carmichael called down the barn aisle from the tack room. "If not, hurry up. Ms Phillips is eager to get started. Today's going to be your first chance to put some of the dressage we've been practising to music."

"Why's Ms Phillips teaching us?" Abigail called out from Hardy's stall. "I thought today was a lesson with you."

Honey had just been thinking the same thing. Normally Ms Carmichael taught their Friday afternoon riding class.

"Yeah," Lynsey added as she adjusted Quest's bridle. "Ms Phillips is supposed to be the jumping coach. What does she know about dressage?"

"Quite a bit, actually," Ms Carmichael replied. "But the reason she's teaching you today is because she's the one who volunteered to take the training course for the new module. She's very excited to put everything she's learned into practice."

"Cool," Dylan said, giving a gentle tug on Morello's reins to get him moving. The skewbald gelding put his ears back, then finally moved forward into the aisle. "Come on, Morello. Time for you to learn to dance!"

Soon the entire class was warming up in the ring. Honey started by asking Minnie to do some lateral work at the walk. The mare felt calm and willing, moving forward into a trot at the slightest nudge from her rider's calves.

"Good girl," Honey murmured. Riding the beautiful grey pony was her greatest pleasure in the world. She glanced gratefully towards Dylan, who had made it all possible by convincing her parents to buy Minnie and loan her to Honey.

Dylan looked a lot less pleased than Honey felt. She was frowning as she struggled to keep her pony from drifting crookedly off the track. "Knock it off, Morello!" she exclaimed. "It's not the best day for one of your cranky moods." She paused, clearly considering what she'd just said as Morello drifted even further in towards the centre. "Not that there's ever a good day for that, unless it's a day I'm not going to be riding at all."

Ms Phillips heard her and laughed. "Never mind, Dylan," she said. "Morello may be cranky, but he's moving well. You just need to figure out how to communicate in a way that'll convince him to do what you want." She stepped over and grabbed a thick packet of papers from a chair outside the ring and flipped through it. "All right. Now that everyone's warmed up, let's get started. Today will be your first chance to put your theory and basics into practice with some actual dressage to music."

"So what kind of music are we talking about?" Lani asked. "Maybe a little old-school country and western, like Johnny Cash or something? Colorado might like that."

Lynsey let out a snort. "Please!" she spat out. "I'm not riding to some hillbilly anthem about pickup trucks or whatever. Blue doesn't—" She cut herself off, glancing down at the horse she was riding. "Er, I mean, Quest doesn't like that garbage. He prefers top forty."

"Me too," Paris McKenzie put in. "I mean, Whisper too."

"No way!" Dylan said. "Quest told me he likes gangsta rap, actually." She pointed to Paris's pony, a pretty grey mare a little smaller than Minnie. "And Whisper prefers heavy metal. It's her deepest, darkest secret."

"How about some classic rock?" Abigail called out. "I'm pretty sure Hardy is into that."

Her friend Jennifer giggled. "Yeah, Hardy definitely seems like that kind of horse," she agreed.

"It's nice to know our horses have such eclectic musical tastes," Ms Phillips said with a smile. "But I'm afraid they're just going to have to make do with classical." Tucking the training manual under one arm, she stepped over to a stereo set up on a small table at the centre of the ring. "Now, when I turn the music on, I want you all to take the rail tracking left and pick up a walk."

"That's it?" Lynsey said with a sniff. "We don't need music to do that."

"Would you let her finish?" Dylan snapped.

"Would you like to make me?" Lynsey taunted in return.

"Girls!" Ms Phillips said sternly. "Enough, OK? Now, as I was about to say, the first part of this particular piece should match up well with a medium walk. See if you can get your horse's gait to match the rhythm. When the pace of the music changes, you should change with it. If it seems like a trot rhythm, go ahead and trot. Ditto for canter. But only if you're sure the pace of the music fits. Got it?"

Honey nodded eagerly. "Sounds like fun," she commented, gathering up Minnie's reins.

"Yeah," Lynsey muttered. "A blast."

Ms Phillips hit play and music poured out of the portable stereo. The classical piece had a light, rhythmic sound. At first Minnie's walk lagged behind the beat, but Honey pulsed each of her legs in turn, encouraging the mare to step out a little more quickly. Within a few strides, Minnie's hooves were touching down in perfect rhythm with the music. Honey felt her own body moving with the mare's steady four-beat gait – one, two, three, four, one, two, three, four. . .

Then the music changed tempo. *Trot*, Honey thought as soon as she heard the quicker two-beat rhythm. As if reading her mind, Minnie swung into a steady, reaching trot. It took only the tiniest adjustment to get her pace to match the music exactly.

"Brilliant!" Honey murmured under her breath. It was amazing how merely playing some music seemed to add a whole new feeling to riding!

She chanced a brief look around to see how the rest of the class was faring. Tybalt had his head up and his trot was too quick for the tempo, but Malory was working with him, half halting and talking soothingly to settle him down. Lynsey had Quest trotting along briskly in time to the music, and Hardy, Flight and Whisper were all at least coming close to matching the correct pace as well. Morello still looked cranky and his trot was a little slow, but otherwise he and Dylan were doing OK.

Things weren't going too well for Lani, however. Honey could see that Colorado was pulling against her hands and his gait kept bobbling as he tried over and over to break to canter. In the process, his trot had become far too fast for the music and Lani kept having to circle him to stop from running into the other horses. He ended up shaking his head and skittering sideways more than forward.

Then the music changed again, pulling Honey's attention back to her own riding. This time the shift was to a three-beat tempo. She paused just long enough to make sure Minnie was on the bit, then asked for a canter.

The mare responded instantly, gliding into a balanced canter. Sometimes Honey found it difficult to adjust her own movements when going from trot to canter; when that happened she rose for a few strides until she could catch the right rhythm. But having the music as a guide seemed to help her, and this time her hips swung right along with the pony's body, carrying her into the canter as easily as she went from walk to trot.

Wow, she thought, feeling a smile growing on her face as she and Minnie cantered around the ring in time to the song. *I guess maybe there's more to this exercise than just having fun riding to music. It forces us to pay attention to making clean and prompt transitions and adjusting the speed of our horses' gaits as well.*

It made her enjoy the lesson even more to realize that Minnie seemed to be enjoying herself, too. The mare seemed to respond to the music almost as quickly as Honey did. It felt as if they were truly dancing!

Meanwhile, her friends were still having trouble. Morello seemed willing to trot all day long; every time Dylan asked him to canter, he merely sped up into a faster and faster trot. Before long they were passing some of the cantering horses on the inside, and both girl and pony had sour looks on their faces. As for Colorado, he decided to throw in a couple of hops and tiny bucks that Honey was pretty sure were *not* aligned with anything in the soothing classical piece!

When the music finished, Ms Phillips clapped. "Good job, people!" she called out, hurrying over to stop the recording. "Most of you did pretty well for your first attempt."

"Yeah, except me," Dylan said breathlessly. "I have no idea why Morello doesn't feel like cantering today – usually it's his favourite gait! And that fast trot he kept doing every time I asked didn't work with the music very well. Or with my butt, either."

Lani laughed. "Don't worry, Walsh," she said. "At least you only had trouble with one gait. Colorado and I couldn't get our act together for any of the three."

"No kidding," Lynsey put in caustically. "I could barely focus on the music, since I was so busy trying to stay out of your way while that cowpony thing was bucking around the ring."

"Sorry about that," Lani said with a shrug. "But I guess it just shows that Colorado and I really are a perfect match. I have two left feet, and he has four!"

Ms Phillips chuckled. "Never mind, Lani," she said. "Better luck next time. Paris, nicely done with Whisper. And Malory, it looked like Tybalt got better and better as we went along."

"He did," Malory said, her face glowing with pride as she leaned forward to rub Tybalt in front of the withers.

"I think the music might have actually calmed him down a little."

Honey smiled. "Maybe you should get him his own iPod," she joked.

After one more attempt at the same exercise, Ms Phillips told them it was time to move on to trying to put together something closer to a real dressage test to the music. First she divided the class into two groups, then outlined a simple routine consisting of circles, figures of eight, and serpentines as well as various transitions among all three gaits.

"All right, we'll try it one group at a time," she said. "Honey, Paris, Malory, Jennifer, you four can go first. Hang on, let me find the right music..."

Soon a different classical piece was pouring out of the speakers. Honey found herself in the lead, which made her nervous for a moment. But she nudged Minnie into a walk and started on their first circle. Trying to match Minnie's stride to the beat of the music – not to mention trying to remember which move came next – distracted her from her self-consciousness, and soon she forgot there was anyone in the ring at all aside from her and Minnie. Before she knew it, they'd finished with a halt and salute at X.

"Wonderful!" Ms Phillips cried. "Honey, you seem to have a real knack for this."

"Way to go, Honey!" Dylan cheered as the rest of the second group whooped and clapped with enthusiasm. Well, all except for Lynsey, who just sat slumped in her saddle picking at her nails and looking bored.

"Thanks." Honey couldn't stop grinning as she leaned down to pat her horse. "But it's really down to Minnie. She's the best!"

"Ugh," Lani said with a shudder. "I thought Lynsey was going to murder me when Colorado spooked and we ended up cutting her off in the middle of that last figure of eight."

"Forget her," Dylan advised, her words slightly garbled thanks to the several open safety pins she was holding in her mouth. "And hold still. I don't want to prick you again. For one thing, Rosie'll kill me if we get blood on her dress."

"Do you want me to hold those?" Honey suggested, staring at the pins. "If you swallow them and have to be rushed away to hospital, I'm not sure Malory and I have got the fashion eye to finish helping Lani get ready."

Dylan spat the pins out in her own palm and set them on the desk beside her. All four friends were in the dorm room shared by Lani and Honey. Normally Lani's side looked a bit messy, while Honey's was neat as a pin. However, at the moment the entire place looked as if a tornado had just gone through it. Open fashion magazines and articles of clothing covered every surface – floor, beds, dressers – while random bits of jewellery and make-up were scattered across both desktops.

"It's OK, I'm done," Dylan said, stepping back and surveying Lani with satisfaction. "She looks fabulous!"

"Thanks." Lani sounded dubious as she glanced down

at herself. She was wearing a borrowed three-quarter-length purple dress and a pair of silver high-heeled sandals. "I just hope Dr Duffy recognizes me when he comes to pick me up."

Honey hoped Sam would have the sense to dress up a bit instead of showing up in his favourite jeans and trainers. She'd meant to call him after riding class to make sure, but the girls had been rushed putting their ponies away and had barely had time to feed them a few carrots before having to bolt back to the dorm to help Lani get ready for the science fair award ceremony that evening.

Never mind, Honey told herself. *Dr Duffy will probably pick Sam up at St Kit's on the way to the ceremony. If Sam isn't properly turned out, he can just send him back inside to change.*

"All right, here's your purse," Dylan told Lani, digging under a pile of discarded dresses and coming up with a sparkly silver clutch, which she shoved into Lani's hands. "Now let me touch up your lips."

"I feel like some kind of Barbie doll." Lani was doing her best to keep her lips still as she spoke, since Dylan was busy smearing vast quantities of gloss on to them. "The award people are probably expecting me to show up in a lab coat or something anyway."

"You're the glamorous side of science, that's all!" Dylan capped the gloss, gave Lani one last satisfied look-over, and then turned to Honey. "OK, come on," she said. "Your turn now."

Honey blinked. "Me? What do you mean?"

Lani smiled and stepped over to her. "Yes, you," she said, putting an arm around Honey and squeezing. "I get to bring a guest along tonight, remember? And you're it."

Honey gasped. "Really? But I thought—"

"No time for thought right now," Dylan said briskly. "Now hurry up and let's get you looking glamorous, too."

"Are you sure we have time for this?" Honey asked anxiously as Dylan worked on her blonde hair with a curling iron some fifteen minutes later. "I don't want to make Lani late for her big night."

"Don't worry, there's plenty of time." Lani grabbed Malory's arm to check her watch. "OK, maybe not plenty. But some."

"Good thing I'm an expert at getting awesome outfits put together in record time," Dylan put in, shifting the curling iron to another lock of Honey's hair.

Malory laughed. "That's because you've had so much practice," she teased. "You never wake up until thirty seconds before you're due in class."

Dylan shot her a look. "Are you going to stand there insulting me, or would you rather help out by finding that peach lipgloss that looks so good on Honey?"

"I'm on it." Malory sprang into action, digging through the cosmetics on Honey's desk.

Honey just sat back and let her friends do their thing. She still couldn't believe Lani had chosen her to come along to the science award dinner. As much as she knew Sam would have enjoyed spending the evening with Lani, Honey was thrilled that she had been invited. It would be amazing to see her friend receive her award.

And it was so cool of her to surprise me with it like this, and for Dylan and Mal to help, she thought, pursing her lips as Malory came at her with the lipgloss. *I really do have the greatest friends in the world.*

In less time than she would have believed possible, Honey was ready to go. Dylan had produced a cute scarlet dress for her to wear, with a short flippy skirt and a matching bolero jacket. A scarlet headband completed the look, along with Honey's favourite satin ballet flats.

"Fab!" Dylan pronounced, stepping back and surveying both Honey and Lani. "You two are going to be the belles of the ball."

"Now hurry up," Malory added. "Dr Duffy should be here any second."

Sure enough, the science teacher was just stepping into the Adams lobby when the girls hurried down the curving staircase. He looked surprisingly dapper in a black tuxedo, his normally wild brown hair slicked back and tidy.

"Well, don't you two look nice!" he called out with a smile as Lani and Honey came towards him.

"You too, Dr D," Lani said. "How come you don't dress like that for class?"

The teacher chuckled. "Maybe I should start – might surprise some of my students enough to make them stay awake for my lectures," he joked back, shooting Dylan a wink. "Now come on, you two, we'd better shake a leg. We don't want the guest of honour to be late for her own party!"

"Thanks again for inviting me," Honey told Lani as they both dug into their desserts.

"Thanks for coming," Lani replied. "It means a lot to have you here. I mean, I wish Dyl and Mal could've come too, of course. But it was really no contest when I had to choose one person for this. You were so supportive when I was putting this project together. In fact, I think you were the only one who didn't try to convince me to blow it off every time movie night rolled around!"

Honey smiled. "It's easy to be supportive when you're supporting someone so brilliant."

"Oh, go on!" Lani waved a hand. Then she grinned. "Well? Didn't you hear me? Go on! Tell me more about how brilliant I am!"

Both girls were still giggling when Dr Duffy leaned over from his seat beside Lani. "Heads up, girls," he whispered. "I think Lani's big moment is coming soon – you don't want to miss your cue."

The award ceremony had been a lot of fun so far. Lani had been wrong about one thing – it wasn't being held in the state capital of Richmond after all. Instead, the state's science board members had arranged for the event to take place at a grand country hotel on the far side of Cheney Falls. It seemed as if every science teacher in the state was there, along with all sorts of school administrators and others. The evening had started with drinks and canapés, followed by a speech from the witty, personable host of a science-oriented show on TV. Even though Honey wasn't nearly as interested in science as Lani, she found the talk both fascinating and entertaining.

"And now, time for the main event," the TV host said, bounding back on to the stage. "The state science board has asked me to do the honours tonight, so without further ado, let's have a round of applause for this year's winner of the Virginia Student Science Trophy – Miss Lani Hernandez!"

Honey cheered and applauded wildly as Lani stood up, grinning self-consciously and waving to the crowd. Dr Duffy pumped his fist and added a loud "Whoop whoop!" to the cheers. Lani laughed and "whoop whooped" back at him, then turned and jogged up the steps to the little stage at the end of the banquet room.

"Congratulations, Miss Hernandez." The TV host handed over the trophy, a crystal double helix. "Would you like to say a few words?"

"Sure." Lani hoisted the trophy for a better look. "Wow, this thing is cool!"

That made everyone laugh. "Speech! Speech!" Dr Duffy called out.

Lani grinned. "OK, I guess that means I need to thank my super-awesome science teacher at Chestnut Hill, Dr Duffy. You're the coolest!" She pointed towards Dr Duffy, who stood up and took a little bow. "I'd also like to thank my family and friends," Lani went on. "I wish they could all be here tonight. But at least I have my best friend with me – Honey Harper. Stand up, Honey!"

Blushing wildly, Honey climbed to her feet and looked around. Everyone was looking at her, smiling and clapping. It was a little embarrassing, but also kind of nice. It reminded her of the curtain calls after the plays she'd been in back in England.

"You're the coolest, too, Honey," Lani said, blowing her a kiss. "I definitely couldn't have done it without you. Thanks for being there!"

"You're welcome," Honey said automatically. She was pretty sure Lani couldn't hear her over all the clapping. But she was also pretty sure she knew.

"Check it out," Lani called, taking one hand off Colorado's reins to point through a grove of budding dogwoods just off the trail. "I think I just saw a robin!"

"Where?" Malory asked, peering around to catch a glimpse of the bird.

"I see it too! That makes it official," Dylan said. "It must be spring!"

Honey could believe that. It was Saturday morning and the four friends were enjoying a trail ride through the rolling, wooded hills that made up much of Chestnut Hill's sprawling campus. Minnie seemed to be having as good a time as her rider. The grey pony's trot was as smooth as silk, and Honey found herself humming the classical piece they'd ridden to in class the day before.

Dylan heard her and glanced over. "Uh oh," she said.

49

"I recognize that tune. Does this mean you're going to turn this trail ride into a musical dressage lesson?"

"You heard what Sam said about Honey's acting past," Lani warned. "Is it any wonder Minnie is stagestruck, too?"

"Maybe we should see if they can both join the school drama club," Malory joked.

Dylan scratched her chin thoughtfully. "I wonder if a horse would fit on the stage in the auditorium?" she asked with mock seriousness.

Honey just laughed. "Very funny, you guys," she said. "Anyway, if there's anyone who was meant to be on stage, it's Lani. You should have heard her acceptance speech last night."

"Yeah," Lani said. "It's just lucky I didn't have to dance. Otherwise I probably would've fallen off the stage."

"That's OK." Dylan grinned. "With all those science types there, they could've used that as an excuse to study the effects of gravity or something."

Malory gathered up Tybalt's reins. "Come on, you guys, it's the weekend! Are we going to talk about dressage and science, or are we going to canter?"

"This meeting of the Adams House Get Crafty club will now come to order!" Dylan announced, tapping the table in the common room with a hoof pick she'd produced from the pocket of her jeans.

Lani rolled her eyes. "Very official, Madame Not-President," she said. Then she glanced around the table, where about a dozen Adams House residents were gathered. "OK, everybody, should we get started?"

"That's what we're here for!" sophomore Hayley Cousins said.

Her friend Ansty Van Sweetering nodded. "I thought Honey was the president of this club. Was there a coup I didn't hear about?"

Honey smiled. "No coup," she said. "I just happen to have some very talkative friends."

"No kidding," eighth-grader Razina Jackson agreed with a laugh. "If the government could harness the power of Dylan and Lani's mouths, we wouldn't have an energy crisis any more."

Dylan stuck out her tongue at Razina. "Nice," she said. "You're not exactly shy and retiring yourself, you know."

"Enough," Honey broke in. "I'm calling this meeting to order, all right? Now let's talk about what we want our next club project to be. We still have heaps of materials left over from our Valentine's Day session, plus our sponsor has sent us some more stuff this week."

"Sponsor?" Faith Holby-Travis echoed, sounding mystified. Honey had noticed that the petite, pretty freshman sounded that way a lot. Faith was a very talented cellist and tended not to notice much outside of the world of music.

"Matilda Harvey – remember her?" Malory put in. "She runs the craft shop near my dad's store in Cheney Falls."

"Oh, right," a seventh-grader named Ceci Ortega

said. "I remember her. She came to help us with those holiday ornaments we made for the dorm charity project last term."

Now almost all the heads were nodding around the table, including Faith's. "OK, so what's our next project going to be?" asked Alexandra Cooper, Malory's room-mate.

"We could always stick with the holiday theme and do something for the start of spring," Lani suggested.

"Or Easter," senior Rachel Goodhart put in. "Or maybe Arbor Day – when is that, anyway?"

Dylan wrinkled her nose. "We don't want to get stuck in a holiday rut," she said. "Why not think outside the box this time?"

"Like how?" Alexandra asked.

Dylan shrugged. "I was hoping one of you would have some genius ideas."

"I know – we could make some banners or pom poms or something to support the lacrosse team," Rachel suggested eagerly. She was the captain of the school's senior team, which had recently started its season.

"I don't know," Malory said dubiously. "Seems kind of a narrow focus."

Razina laughed. "Yeah," she added. "Besides, if we do that, the next thing you know the horse freaks among us will be having us making handmade wreaths to hang around their horses' necks while they ride or something." She shot a mischievous look at the riders in the bunch.

"Ooh!" Dylan brightened, brandishing her hoof pick. "I like that!"

"I'm not so sure," Lani said, glancing at Malory. "Can you imagine how Tybalt would react to having a wreath hung around his neck?"

Malory shuddered. "I don't even want to try," she joked. "But listen – instead of focusing on just one school team, why not do something to support all of them? Like, um, I don't know. . ." She glanced over at Honey for help.

"What about something to do with school spirit in general?" Honey said. "We could do a banner to hang up for games and horse shows. . ."

"I guess," Faith said, leaning her elbows on the table. "But what about those of us who don't ride or play any other sports?"

"'Those of us?'" Rachel echoed. "You mean you?"

"Or what about some sort of art piece that could be displayed in Old House?" Honey said quickly, not wanting the meeting to degenerate into an argument between the two girls. "A poster, or a collection of photographs – oh! I know. Perhaps a collage."

"A collage?" Ansty sounded interested. "What do you mean? What kind of collage?"

Honey brushed back a stray strand of hair and glanced around the table. "I was thinking of something that might capture all of what we love about going to school here," she said. "It could include the teams and such, but also other things like arts clubs and performance groups and academic stuff, plus just general school life. We could use photographs and drawings and maybe some poems or something, plus other materials – you know, a scrap of fabric showing school colours, a beaded image of a team mascot, and whatever other items represent other bits of this school."

"I get it," Alexandra chimed in. "It would be sort of like a giant scrapbook page about Chestnut Hill."

"I like that!" Hayley said. "If it turns out well, maybe it could even be printed on the cover of the school magazine."

Heads were nodding all around the table. "I could take some pictures at our lacrosse match this weekend," Rachel volunteered.

"Fantastic," Honey said, grabbing a piece of paper and starting to take notes.

"It would be cool if we could add some special digital effects to some of the photos," Ceci put in. "Like different colour palettes or whatever."

"Definitely!" Rachel agreed. "You're good with computers, right? Let's meet up at the student centre after the match and see what we can come up with."

Ceci nodded happily, seeming thrilled at the idea of hanging out with the popular upperclassman. "I'll be there," she promised Rachel.

"Even though this is an Adams project, there should probably be representation of all the houses," Hayley said. "Maybe we could do the names of each in beads or glitter, then ask for at least one photo from each house showing their dorm pride."

"Good idea," Honey said, jotting it down. "But we shouldn't only focus on the dorms – we also want to show the whole campus." She smiled as she thought about that trail ride through the woods earlier in the day. "For instance, to show how beautiful this place is, we could collect some spring leaves or other natural items out in the woods."

"Ooh, that'll be amazing!" Razina said. "I'm not doing anything tomorrow – I'll go out and look for that kind of stuff if you want."

"I'll come with you," Alexandra offered. "We can go right after brunch."

Soon everyone was buzzing with ideas. They came so fast and furious that Honey had trouble keeping up as she scribbled notes.

"This is great," she said at last, once the torrent of ideas finally slowed to a trickle. "I think everyone knows what they've got to do. Let's meet again next week or the week after and start putting things together. Meeting adjourned."

Everyone stood up and gathered their things, still chatting about the project. Honey and her three best friends drifted towards the door behind the others.

"This is going to be great," Lani told Honey. "I wasn't sure this craft club was going to fly, but I'm psyched to do the collage!"

"Me too," Malory agreed. "It's a great idea, Honey."

Dylan reached over and gave Honey a hug. "Yeah," she agreed. "Leave it to our Honey to figure out a way to totally capture the spirit of Chestnut Hill!"

"Try it again," Ms Phillips called, hurrying over to rewind the music on the stereo. "That was better, but I'd still like to see crisper halt-trot transitions with no steps of walk in between. Otherwise you end up missing the musical cue."

"Wow, this dancing on horseback stuff is harder than it looks," Dylan puffed to Honey.

It was Monday afternoon and Honey and her classmates were having another musical dressage lesson. This time Ms Phillips had made the pattern they were supposed to follow much more difficult, with lots of transitions and more complicated figures.

"Don't blame me for our sloppy transitions," Lynsey told the instructor with a sniff and a disdainful glance down at Quest. "This horse simply isn't as well-trained as Bluegrass."

Ms Phillips raised her eyebrows. "All right, Lynsey. Just do your best," she said. "It will help – and I'm talking to all of you – if you really listen to the music and try to absorb it. Not just the beat, but the feel and the character of it. If you can really get it, it should show in your performance." She looked at Honey with a smile. "If you're not sure what I'm talking about, just watch Honey and Minnie. You'll see that the music seems to flow through the pair of them – it shows in how Honey rides, and in Minnie's gaits as well."

"Teacher's pet," Lani teased with a wink.

Honey blushed. "Thanks, Ms Phillips," she said. "I think having the music to focus on actually makes me ride better."

"I think you're right," the teacher agreed. "Keep it up, Honey. Now let's take it again from the top, everyone!"

They ran through the programme one more time. Honey found herself lost in the music as always, riding more by instinct than by thought. Minnie was always agreeable, but the more they rode to music, the more responsive the little mare seemed to get. They ended the exercise exactly on cue, with Minnie standing square and alert and Honey sitting proudly in the saddle.

"Bravo, everyone!" Ms Phillips clapped. "Lynsey, your transitions were much better that time."

Lynsey shrugged, fiddling with her reins. "I guess," she muttered. "We still blew the second serpentine, though."

Honey shot Lynsey a look. She couldn't believe she was still complaining about Quest. From what Honey had noticed during her own ride, it had seemed that the pair had done very well.

Lynsey's so caught up in feeling sorry for herself because Blue's injured that she can't even see that she should be proud of herself, Honey thought with a touch of sadness. *A lot of people might think Lynsey got where she is because she has such a talented pony, but she truly is a gifted rider. Quest isn't easy to ride, and she's done brilliantly with him so far. . .*

She shook off the thoughts, not wanting to miss Ms Phillips's other comments. After critiquing each rider's performance, the coach called for them all to give it one more try before calling it a day.

Halfway through the programme, Honey was trotting along the short side when she noticed movement in the bleachers just outside the ring. Glancing that way, she saw Ms Carmichael sitting down to watch. Then the music changed, and she turned her attention back to Minnie, asking for the next transition.

When the music ended this time, there were two people applauding – Ms Phillips and Ms Carmichael. The riding director climbed down from her seat and hurried over, ducking under the rail to join the jumping coach in the centre of the ring.

"Very impressive, everyone!" Ms Carmichael said. "I can see that Ms Phillips is doing a good job with this module so far." She shot the other instructor a smile.

"Thanks," Lani called out. "She did a great job choreographing that spook and fart move Colorado and I performed this time, didn't she?"

Ms Carmichael chuckled. "This is supposed to be a learning experience, Lani," she said. "Nobody expects you to be perfect."

"Good thing," Lynsey muttered, rolling her eyes.

Ms Carmichael didn't seem to hear her. "Honey, Paris, Jennifer," she said. "I'd like you three to stay after class today. I need to talk to you about something."

"OK," Honey said as the other two girls nodded. She couldn't imagine what the riding director wanted to speak to the three of them about, but she wasn't too concerned. Based on the pleasant expression on Ms Carmichael's face, it was unlikely to be anything bad.

"I'll finish grooming Minnie for you if you want," Malory offered about twenty minutes later, sticking her head over the mare's half-door. "You'd better scoot – the other two just left for Ms Carmichael's office."

Honey glanced up, hoof pick in hand. "Oh!" she exclaimed. "I nearly forgot!"

She had been so pleased with Minnie's performance in that day's lesson that she'd lingered over her post-ride grooming longer than usual. Now she realized she'd lost track of time.

Just then Dylan appeared beside Malory. "Go," she ordered. "We'll pamper Minnie within an inch of her life for you, don't worry."

"Thanks." Honey smiled at them. "If I'm not back before you leave, I'll meet you back at the dorm."

She gave Minnie one last pat, then let herself out of the stall and hurried up the barn aisle. Halfway to the stable block where Ms Carmichael's office was located, she caught up with Paris and Jennifer.

"There you are." Paris greeted her with a shrug. "We thought you must've already left."

"What do you think she wants with us?" Jennifer sounded a little nervous. "I forgot to wipe my bit down straight after class last week, but I thought I'd remembered before she noticed."

Honey smiled at the younger girl. "Don't worry," she said. "I doubt it's anything like that. Ms Carmichael didn't seem angry."

They were almost to the office by now. Ms Carmichael was coming out of the converted stall when she spotted them.

"Ah, there you are," she said. "I was just coming to look for you. I wanted to talk to you three separately about whether you'd be willing to help out at the next All Schools League show over at St Kit's."

"Of course," Honey said right away. "What do you need help with? Bathing and grooming beforehand?"

"Not this time," Ms Carmichael said. "We've agreed to put on a display of dressage to music to show the rest of the schools how the module is going. After watching part of your lesson today, I think you three would be just the riders to do it."

Paris gasped. "Really?" she exclaimed. "Us?" She sounded flattered and a little shocked. Honey was feeling much the same way.

"Are you sure?" she asked. "I mean, I know Minnie is brilliant, but I'm hardly the most experienced rider in the group. Malory. . ."

"Malory did very well, too," Ms Carmichael broke in. "But she'll be busy captaining the junior jumping team. Besides, I happen to think it will make quite a nice show with your three beautiful grey mares performing together."

Honey nodded, realizing the riding director was right. While either Malory or Lynsey would be likely to perform just as well as or better than she, Paris and Jennifer would, they would both be busy with the jumping team at the show. So would Dylan, who had been doing better lately with Morello in the dressage unit.

"What do you say?" Ms Carmichael smiled at the three of them. "Want to give it a try?"

"I guess so," Jennifer said. "But do you really think we'll be good enough by then? The show's next Saturday, right?"

"Don't worry," Ms Carmichael said. "You'll be doing a routine very similar to the one you practised today. And I'll make sure you have plenty of extra practice time with Ms Phillips this week to get ready."

Honey felt a thrill of nerves in the pit of her stomach, but she nodded. How could she say no to the opportunity to show everyone what a fantastic horse Minnie was?

"I'm in," she said.

"Oh wow!" Lani exclaimed. "This is going to be so cool. You and Minnie are going to be amazing, Honey!"

"I hope so." Honey glanced at Minnie's stall. The sociable pony had her head hanging out over the half-door, her ears pricked in their direction. "I mean, I know Minnie will be perfect, but I hope I don't get nervous at having so many people watching and mess up."

"You won't," Malory assured her. "It'll be just like being on stage again. Remember? Like Sam was telling us."

"Right!" Dylan put in. "What show was it again?"

"*Annie Get Your Gun*," Lani supplied. Then she launched into the chorus of one of the songs. Honey laughed and joined in.

The other two did as well. It was obvious that Malory didn't know the words, but she did her best to hum along. Dylan even grabbed a broom standing against a wall and started dancing around the aisle with it.

"What's going on in here?" asked Kelly, peering out from the tack room.

"We're just – oops!" When Dylan turned her head to respond, she forgot to look where she was going and stepped into a half-full water bucket sitting in the aisle. She tripped and caught herself on a stack of straw bales. The water bucket wasn't so lucky. It went flying, spraying its contents everywhere.

"Thanks a lot, Dylan!" Kelly sounded dismayed as she hurried towards them and grabbed the now-empty bucket before it could roll into Colorado's stall. "I didn't have anywhere near enough work to do today – now I'll be mopping up so that water doesn't turn the aisle into an ice rink if it freezes tonight."

"Sorry," Dylan said contritely. "Want us to stick around and help?"

The stable hand's expression softened. "Nah, it's no

biggie," she said. "Just get out of here before you manage to knock down the whole barn, OK?"

"Deal. Thanks, Kelly, and sorry again – I owe you one." Dylan scooted for the exit. "Come on, guys. I think I hear our dinner calling."

That evening after dinner Honey called her parents to tell them her news. "We're so proud of you, Honey!" her mother exclaimed. "You always did love performing, after all – I'm sure you'll do a brilliant job of it."

"Indeed," Mr Harper added. "See that Lani takes lots of photos, will you? We'll be expecting to see a full photo essay afterwards."

"Oh," Honey said, taken aback. "But I was hoping you might come watch in person. The show's at St Kit's so Sam will be there, too."

"I wish we could," her mother said sadly. "But I'm afraid we have a prior engagement this Saturday that we won't be able to get out of."

Honey was disappointed, but she tried to swallow it. Her parents were always supportive of everything she and Sam did; if they said they couldn't make it, it meant they really couldn't.

"Do you have a wedding or something to attend?" she asked. "I understand. This is all kind of last minute."

"We'd better get off the phone," her father said. "Sorry we won't be able to come watch you in person. But do let us know how your practices are going this week, all right?"

"Sure," Honey said. "Love you both."

"Us too," her mother said. "Talk to you later, darling."

"Tempo, Jennifer!" Ms Phillips called, clapping her hands in time with the music. "You're falling behind."

"Sorry!" Jennifer called back breathlessly, urging her pony forward. "It's just that Flight's so much shorter than the other two, it's like she has to take two steps for every one of theirs just to keep up."

Honey looked back, trying to gauge how far behind Flight had fallen. Taking a stronger hold on Minnie's reins, she tried to shorten the mare's stride without changing the tempo to give Jennifer a chance to catch up. Minnie obeyed, though Paris was having more trouble with Whisper, who appeared to be trying to evade the bit and turn into the centre of the ring.

Riding to the music by yourself is one thing, Honey thought, struggling to recall whether they were meant to slow to walk at C or do another twenty-metre circle first. *But getting everything to happen at the same time on three different ponies is a lot more tricky!*

It was Tuesday evening. The girls were having their first official practice for the dressage display. It was almost dark, so they were riding in the indoor ring, where Ms Phillips had set out a dressage ring with chains and printed letters to help guide them.

"Oops!" Paris cried out as she fell out of line. "Sorry, I thought we were supposed to do a serpentine there. Aren't we?"

"Nope," Jennifer called out, her voice bouncing in

time with her pony's working trot. "That's on the other side. Isn't it?"

"I think so." Honey frowned, trying to remember.

"Hang on – let's stop and reorganize," Ms Phillips said, turning off the music. "You're riding well, and I know you can perform all the movements. I think you're just having a bit of trouble staying together."

Honey nodded, rolling her head around on her neck to stretch it out as Minnie drifted to a halt. "That's for sure," she said. "I feel as if my head's going to fall off from trying to keep an eye on the others all the time!"

The coach smiled sympathetically. "That's all right, it's a learning curve," she said. "But listen, don't feel you have to keep the others in view all the time. That goes for all three of you." She glanced at Paris and Jennifer. "Instead, look where you're going just as you always would and try to listen for the other ponies' footfalls instead. If you do that and make sure to stay with the beat, things should work out fine."

Paris nodded. "I'll try," she said, sounding a bit frustrated. "I just hope Whisper will try to remember what a half halt is instead of doing her best to catch up with Minnie."

"She's a good mare, and very well-trained," Ms Phillips reminded her kindly. "If you keep practising, I think you'll both do fine. Now – shall we try it again from the top?"

By the time Honey staggered out of the stable area an hour later, her legs were aching and her neck was stiff. Despite the coach's instructions, it had been difficult to resist the temptation to check on the other two riders from time to time. Still, Ms Phillips had seemed pleased with their last run-through, giving Honey hope that they wouldn't completely embarrass themselves on Saturday.

There was no sign of her friends back at the dorm, so after changing out of her riding clothes, Honey called Dylan's Blackberry. It turned out that the other three were studying over at the student centre.

"I'll be right there," Honey said. "If my legs will carry me that far, that is."

"Tough practice, huh?" Dylan sounded sympathetic. "I know the feeling. Ms Carmichael always works us extra hard before a competition, too."

When Honey arrived, the student centre was packed. Dylan, Lani and Malory had staked out a couple of computers at one end of the row. Malory was composing an English essay, Lani was checking her email, and Dylan was sitting at a table beside the computer stations working on a sketch of Morello that she wanted to include in their Get Crafty collage.

"Need a computer?" Lani asked, glancing up. "You can have this one."

"No, it's OK." Honey flopped down next to Dylan. "I'm mostly caught up. I just have to read a couple of chapters of history."

She opened up the textbook she'd brought. Her head was still ringing with classical music – by now, she knew the piece they were performing to by heart. The words of the US Constitution and pictures of the Philadelphia Convention of 1787 swam in front of her eyes, the solemn-faced delegates, including Benjamin Franklin and George Washington, seeming to dance in time to the music.

"You OK?" Dylan glanced over. "You've been staring at that same page for, like, ten minutes."

Honey blinked and shook her head to clear it. "Guess I'm just distracted," she admitted. "I can't stop thinking about the dressage performance. What if I forget the pattern we're supposed to ride and mess up the whole thing?"

Lani heard her and spun around on her computer chair. "You taught me what to do about that, remember?" she said. "When I couldn't remember my test before our one-day event back in the fall, you told me to sketch out the moves in the dirt. That really helped me."

"Oh, right." Honey had almost forgotten about that tip, which she'd learned from a former riding instructor back in the UK. "It's worth a try, I suppose. Anyone got any paper?"

"Here you go." Malory ripped a page out of her notebook and handed it over.

"Thanks." Pushing her history book aside, Honey bent over the sheet and started sketching the pattern she would be riding on Saturday, humming along as she did. As her pencil ran smoothly over the page, twitching each time there would be a change of pace, Honey realized that she knew the movements much better than she had thought. She relaxed, and felt a tingle of excitement about the performance. *Roll on Saturday!*

7

"Need some help with that?" Honey asked, skidding to a stop upon entering the tack room and seeing Dylan perched on one of the trunks while she struggled to untangle Morello's best show bridle.

Dylan stopped wrestling with the wad of leather just long enough to shoot her a disapproving look. "You're one of the competitors today, not a groom, remember?" she said. "Go do what you need to do. I'll get someone else to save me this time." Glancing out the tack room door, she yelled out, "Hey, Hernandez! Get in here."

Lani was coiling up the water hose at the end of the aisle. When she turned and saw the mess in Dylan's hand, she tossed the rest of the hose on the rack and hurried over. "Coming," she called. "Let me guess, Walsh – you spent so much time cleaning your saddle yesterday that you totally forgot your horse is supposed to wear something on his head, too?"

Dylan grinned weakly. "It's not my fault, honest. The bridle fell off the rack and ended up wedged down behind the bandage box sometime after I last used it. Out of sight, out of mind. . ."

"Excuses, excuses." Lani grabbed the bridle out of her hands. "I'll see if I can get the knots out – you go grab the cleaning stuff. Hey, Honey, do you need something, too?"

"No, I'm all right. Carry on." Honey picked up the travelling boots she'd come for and then hurried back out of the tack room. It felt strange to be one of the competitors on this show morning rather than just helping out. The mayhem and sense of barely controlled panic were much the same, of course. But it was also different now that she was right in the centre of it.

Minnie was hanging her head out when Honey returned to her stall. The mare's snow-white coat gleamed as a result of hours of bathing and grooming. Honey had plaited Minnie's silky mane earlier that morning with help from Malory, who had a knack for such things.

"Wow," Honey murmured as she ducked under the stall guard. "You look perfect!"

Minnie nuzzled Honey's hair, then nosed the pockets of her windbreaker, searching for a treat. Honey smiled and pushed her away gently.

"Easy," she said. "This is my only clean show shirt. If you drool green horse slobber down it, there's no way *I'm* going to look perfect enough to ride you!"

Clipping a lead line on to the mare's leather halter, Honey led her out into the aisle. After picking a few bits of bedding out of her feet, she put on Minnie's thickly-padded travelling boots. She was adjusting the last one when Kelly the stable hand rushed by clutching a clipboard in one hand and a bucket of brushes in the other.

"Honey, there you are," she said, sounding distracted as she paused and gave the pony a quick once-over. "Is Minnie ready to go?"

"She is now." Honey straightened up and brushed off her hands.

"Good. You can go ahead and take her out – the trailer's outside." Kelly consulted her clipboard. "Looks like the junior team is going first, with your demonstration immediately following, so we'll want all of you in the first load."

Honey nodded. Chestnut Hill's horse trailer could accommodate up to six horses at a time. That meant that for away shows, they had to either hire another trailer to haul the rest of the horses or make several trips. Because St Kit's was only a few miles away, today they would be doing the latter.

As the stable hand hurried away, Honey took a deep breath and looked at Minnie, who was standing calmly. So far the morning had been so hectic that Honey hadn't had much chance to feel nervous. But now butterflies were beginning to dance in her stomach.

"Here we go, girl," she whispered to the pony, giving a light tug on the lead rein to get her going.

"I hope I don't forget the entire routine as soon as we start," Jennifer moaned as she fumbled with a plait that

Flight had rubbed out on the short ride over to St Kit's. "Especially that leg yield near the beginning – I always seem to forget about that one."

"You'd better not," Paris joked, sounding as calm as the other girl seemed frantic. "Because if you do, Whisper and I will run right over you."

Honey finished adjusting the hay net she'd hung up for Minnie. The girls had just finished tying their ponies at a wooden hitching rail set up in the shade of St Kit's picturesque stone barn. Morello and Colorado were also there, along with Quest, Skylark and Calvin, the other junior team mounts, who had come separately in a three-horse trailer that belonged to one of Chestnut Hill's teachers. Both trailers had already departed on their way back to the school to pick up more horses.

The show was scheduled to start in about twenty minutes, and all around the barn and arenas the preparations were at a fever pitch. Most of the other visiting schools were working out of their trailers, which were parked in the gravel lot nearby, though several competitors from Two Towers were tied further down the hitching rail. One girl from Allbright's was riding her very tall bay horse around the grassy area at a rapid walk, several times almost crashing into another rider dressed in Lindenwood colours, who appeared to be performing some kind of complicated ground work with her stocky palomino pony. Meanwhile Malory was hand-walking Tybalt in a quieter area behind the parking lot, trying to keep him calm until it was time to start their warm-up.

"Stop," Honey begged her two fellow dressage riders as they continued bickering over the details of the programme. "You're making me nervous! I mean, little shows are one thing, but I've never done anything like this before. I was counting on the two of you to get me back on track if I start to panic and forget everything we're supposed to be doing!"

"Are you kidding?" Jennifer retorted. "I was counting on you! You and Minnie always look as if you both know exactly what you're doing."

Honey shook her head. "Well, Minnie may know what she's doing," she said. "I'm not so sure about me."

Jennifer chuckled sympathetically, but Paris had turned away to stare across the paddock. "Hey, who's that cute guy?" she commented. "He's heading this way! How's my hair?"

Honey turned to follow her gaze and saw Sam coming towards them, weaving his way between clusters of riders and ponies. She smiled, immediately feeling a tiny bit better. Even though her parents couldn't be there to cheer her on, she was very glad that Sam would be. Just seeing him made her feel less nervous. A little bit, anyway.

"That's just my brother," she told the other two girls. "And you can't have him, Paris. Not unless you want to fight off Lani."

"No thanks!" Paris grinned, then turned to fiddle with Whisper's halter.

Sam grinned as Honey slid out from between the ponies to greet him. "There's our own dressage superstar," he quipped, reaching out for a hug. "How's it going?"

Honey wrapped her arms around him, squeezing tightly. "OK, if you don't count me feeling ready to faint with fear at any moment."

"Come on," he said, pulling back and winking at her. "It's just a bit of stage fright. You got the same way before your shows back home, remember?"

Just then Dylan rushed past with a tacked-up Morello in tow. "Wish me luck, guys," she called as she passed. "I'm up sixth."

Malory had just returned with Tybalt. She checked her watch, looking alarmed. "And you're just getting on now?" she squeaked. "I was just about to head to the warm-up ring, and I'm number twelve!"

The two of them hurried off in the direction of the warm-up ring. Sam checked his own watch.

"Oops, I'd better bolt," he said. "I promised Caleb I'd help him get ready before his go." He reached over and squeezed her arm. "Good luck, sis. I'll be watching. Mum and Dad made me promise to take heaps of pictures so they wouldn't completely miss it."

"Just try not to get any shots of me falling off or otherwise making a fool of myself," Honey warned.

"Don't worry." He winked. "If you embarrass yourself too much around here, I'm sure Uncle Harry and Aunt Rose would let you move back to England and live with them."

"Very funny." Honey grinned at him. "See you later."

*

Honey made it over to the viewing stands just in time to see a sleek Appaloosa carrying a St Kit's rider depart the ring after its jumping round while Dylan trotted in for hers. Dylan and Morello did very well, turning in a fast and polished ride with only one scary moment over a spooky vertical decorated with pots of colourful tulips. They ended the round with no faults, and Honey clapped until her hands stung.

Lucy Price and Joanna Boardman also did very well. Lucy and Skylark rode clear, while Joanna's pony Calvin finished with four faults.

Tybalt had trouble at the same vertical as Morello, hesitating, his eyes bugging out at the flowers. But with Malory tactfully but firmly urging him on, he ended up popping over it from nearly a standstill and taking down the top rail with his front feet for four faults. The knockdown seemed to make him extra careful, and he cleared the remaining obstacles with plenty of room to spare. That put him in no danger of any more jumping faults, though it did slow down his time, and the pair ended up with a few time faults as well.

Dylan had cooled Morello down and returned him to the hitching rail following her round. She finished and returned to the stands in time to watch Lynsey's round with Honey and Lani.

"We're tied for second place overall if I'm figuring the scores right," Lani told her as she sat down.

"You probably are," Dylan said. "You're a human calculator." She grinned. "Comes in handy when we're shopping and there's a sale on."

"Only you could think about shopping at a time like this, Walsh," Lani joked. "Well, you and Lynsey, maybe. I guess that's the one thing you two roomies have in common."

Dylan shot her a look of mock horror. "Don't say that," she ordered. "I may be forced to share a bedroom with Lynsey, but other than our room number, we have *nothing* in common!"

"Speaking of Lynsey, she's up next," Honey said. "The last St Kit's rider had time faults, so if Lynsey rides clear, we'll have second place locked up."

Dylan held up her hands, revealing that all of her fingers were crossed. "I normally don't hope for Lynsey to be as perfect as she thinks she is," she said. "But I am today!"

Lynsey rode into the ring looking effortlessly calm. "Wow," Lani commented, leaning forward for a better look. "She and Quest look like a million bucks."

"That's probably how much her saddle cost," Dylan quipped.

Honey watched as Lynsey nodded at the judge and then began her opening circle. Quest trotted around the first quarter of the circle with his head straight up in the air and his ears swivelling anxiously, but he seemed to relax as Lynsey sent him into a canter. They finished the circle and lined up perfectly to the first fence. Quest's ears pricked, and Lynsey sat quietly and waited, folding over him as he cleared it in perfect form.

The next few fences went just as well. Honey found herself holding her breath as the pair cantered around the turn to the last obstacle, an airy white vertical. The distance from the last oxer was a little tricky and had caught a few riders off guard, forcing them to gallop the last two strides and sometimes flatten enough to take down the vertical's top rail.

But Lynsey hardly seemed to move as Quest cantered down to the final fence. His stride was long to begin with, and it lengthened step by step between oxer and vertical. He met the fence in stride, sailing over it with no apparent effort. The Chestnut Hill section of the stands erupted into wild applause and cheering as the pair cantered out through the timers.

"That was awesome!" Dylan shouted, trading high fives with Lani and Honey.

Lani grinned. "Does that mean you admit Lynsey can actually ride even when she's not on her perfect pony?"

"As much as it pains me, yeah, I have to admit it," Dylan said. "The girl can ride, OK?" She shrugged. "But that doesn't mean she's not still annoying."

"Easy, girl," Honey murmured as she and Minnie turned down the centre line at a collected canter. Even as she spoke, she realized it was her own nerves that needed steadying more than her pony's. Minnie hadn't put a foot wrong during their warm-up, performing every bend and transition the moment Honey asked for it. But Honey could feel herself growing nervous again as showtime approached.

Good thing Minnie's not hyper-sensitive like Tybalt, she thought. *Or the type to take advantage like Morello, either.*

Because I'm sure if I were riding either of them in this state, I'd be on the ground by now!

She glanced across one of St Kit's spacious outdoor rings at the other two demo riders. Paris looked cool as a cucumber as she put Whisper through her paces. Jennifer was a little pale, but she was riding well, although Flight looked tenser than usual.

Doing her best not to worry about the others, Honey turned her attention back to her warm-up. Ms Phillips had warned them – as Mr Musgrave had many times before – that it was better not to practise the full test they would be riding too often in case the horses started to anticipate their transitions and perform them too early. That was why they'd mixed things up a bit during their last few practices, often starting the pattern in the middle or riding little bits of it with breaks in between. Once Ms Phillips had even asked them to ride the entire routine in reverse!

So now Honey was careful not to ride more than a couple of moves in sequence – even if she was starting to think that it might not be a bad thing if Minnie knew the pattern. That way she figured the pony could take over if her rider's brain froze up as soon as she rode into the ring!

"Are you guys almost ready?" Malory hurried into the ring followed by Lani and Dylan. "It's nearly time."

Lani nodded. "And the bleachers in the indoor arena are packed – everyone wants to see what you guys are going to do!"

Honey groaned, bringing Minnie to a halt at the rail

where her friends were standing. "Don't say that," she begged. "I'm nervous enough as it is!"

"Forget that," Dylan advised her. "You and Minnie are superstars. You're going to be awesome!"

"That's right." Malory nodded vigorously. "So good luck – we'll be riding with you in spirit!"

With one more chorus of "good lucks", the three of them hurried off to find seats, passing Ms Phillips as she rushed over. "Here we go!" she called. "Gather around, girls."

"Are you sure we can do this?" Jennifer whimpered as she and Paris rode over to join Honey. "I mean, we've only been practising for a week!"

"You'll do fine." Ms Phillips smiled at her, reaching over to give Flight a pat on the neck. "Anyway, this is just a little demonstration, remember? No judges, no pressure. We're just showing everyone how much fun dressage to music can be."

Honey nodded. When she thought about it that way, it seemed a little less daunting. Even so, she tried not to look too hard at the packed stands as the three of them rode into St Kit's spacious indoor arena a few minutes later – though it was difficult to ignore the loud whoops from Dylan and Lani! She and the other riders entered the neatly-groomed dressage ring as Ms Phillips headed for the judges' stand. Picking up the microphone, she gave a brief talk explaining what musical dressage was and why they were putting on this demonstration.

Once again, Honey focused on her pony as she waited for their cue. She rode Minnie around the perimeter of the ring at a brisk trot, allowing the little mare to get a look at the sights. As usual, Minnie was unfazed, though she did take a hard look at a St Kit's banner flapping at the end of the ring. Flight reacted to the flapping banner too, snorting and jumping back when she approached it, but Jennifer managed to steady her and ease her past it without more fuss.

"Good riding," Honey murmured to Jennifer as she rode past. "You're going to do great. Good luck!"

"You too," Jennifer whispered back, sounding nervous but determined as she circled Flight to allow her to see the banner from the other direction.

Then, almost before Honey had time to realize it, the demonstration began. The indoor's overhead lights dimmed and three spotlights came on, illuminating each of the three riders. The music sounded great coming over the school's state-of-the-art sound system. Flight looked a little tense and hollow to begin with, but she soon relaxed into the familiar movements.

As for Honey, her nervousness deserted her as soon as the first notes sounded. She felt her seat melt into the saddle, following Minnie's every move. The little mare arched her neck prettily as if she truly were dancing to the music. Honey was pretty sure she herself had never ridden so well, though she wasted little time thinking about that. She was too busy loving every moment of the experience.

All too soon, it was over. Minnie came to a prompt, square halt on the centre line, with the other two ponies lined up behind her. As the music faded away and the house lights came up, Honey had a big grin on her face. She removed one hand from the reins and dropped it straight down at her side, tipping her head forward in a crisp salute just as they'd practised. A second later, the place erupted in applause.

Wow, that was fun! Honey thought, letting the cheers wash over her as Minnie lifted her head and pricked her dainty ears as if she were curious what all the noise was about. *It's even better than performing on stage!*

"Thank you, girls! That was amazing!" The St Kit's announcer, a tall, skinny senior with a cast on one arm, had taken over the microphone again. He consulted a sheet of paper he was holding. "Let's give it up for Honey Harper, Paris McKenzie, and Jennifer Quinn of Chestnut Hill!"

The cheering grew louder. Even amidst the din, Honey could hear Dylan shouting "Go, Honey!" at the top of her lungs. Searching out her friends and Sam in the crowd, Honey gave them a wave.

A few minutes later the three demo riders were back at the hitching rail, chattering excitedly about the performance as they untacked their ponies. As she replaced Minnie's bridle with her halter and tied her at the rail, Honey noticed Ms Carmichael standing nearby talking with a short, well-dressed man in his fifties. She didn't think much of it, other than to wonder whose father he might be, until Ms Carmichael called her over to join them.

"Honey," the riding director said, "I'd like you to meet Mr James Hutton—"

"Call me Jim," the man broke in, sticking out his hand for Honey to shake. "It's great to meet you, young lady. I'm here at the show to see my son – he's on the St Kit's senior jumping team."

"Oh, I see," Honey said politely. "I hope he does well today."

"Thanks. But that's not what I wanted to talk to you about." The man stuck both hands in his pockets and rocked back on the heels of his loafers. "You see, I'm a director – TV commercials, mostly. And as it happens, we're looking for a dressage rider for a new ad we're shooting for Pegasus Software. And after seeing you ride just now, I think you and your pony would be the perfect fit!"

Honey blinked, not sure she'd heard him right. "M-me?" she said. "And Minnie? In a TV advert?"

"That's right." Mr Hutton pulled a business card out of his pocket. "Here's my card. Your riding director has already agreed to transport you and your horse if you're willing to give it a shot. The time and address are on the back."

Just then the PA system came on again, announcing that the senior team competition was about to start. Mr Hutton glanced towards the jumping ring. "Uh oh, better go get a seat," he said. "Please think about it, Miss Harper. And I hope to see you next Wednesday!"

He hurried off, leaving Honey staring at his card in shock. Ms Carmichael looked nearly as stunned.

At that moment Dylan, Malory and Lani raced

over. "You were great!" Lani cried, grabbing Honey in a big hug.

"Did you hear me cheering for you?" Dylan added. Then she did a double take as she noticed the expression on Honey's face. "Hey, what's going on? You look weird."

Honey blinked and looked up at her. "You'll never believe this," she said. "Minnie and I are going to be on TV!"

It didn't take much to convince Honey's parents to give their permission for her to do the commercial. Ms Carmichael arranged to use the school's smaller horse trailer the following Wednesday, and also checked with Dylan's parents to get their permission for Honey to take Minnie to the shoot, which they gladly granted.

Honey spent Sunday, Monday and Tuesday in a daze. Word spread quickly through the campus that she was about to star in a TV commercial, and fortunately most of her teachers were sympathetic.

"I understand, Honey," her history teacher said after Honey fumbled an answer for the third time in a row. "I did some acting in college myself and could never concentrate on much other than my lines for the week before opening night of a new play." She smiled and winked. "However, I do expect you to snap back into work mode first thing on Thursday."

"I will," Honey promised gratefully. "I swear."

As she left class a few minutes later with her friends, Dylan frowned at her. "I think you've discovered a great new scam, Honey," she said. "Next time I forget to study, I'll just say I've been cast in the lead role of a big-budget Hollywood movie and I'm too nervous to focus on little things like algebra or history."

Lani snorted. "Dream on, Walsh," she said. "No teacher who's ever met you is going to fall for that."

"Why not?" Dylan sounded insulted. "Are you saying I'm not Hollywood starlet material?"

"Not at all," Lani replied. "My point is, you *are* getting-out-of-work-any-way-you-can material, and all of Chestnut Hill knows it!"

Malory laughed. "She's got you there, Dylan."

Dylan shrugged. "Maybe," she said. "But I still think it could work. Just look at how nice all the teachers are being now that Honey's getting ready to be a superstar. Even cranky old Dubois didn't squawk too loudly when she messed up those conjugations in French class this morning!"

Honey shuddered. "Trust me, Dylan, it's not worth it," she said. "I can't even enjoy the break from my studies – I'm far too nervous!"

By Wednesday morning her nerves were stretched so thin she felt as if she were vibrating. She barely remembered getting out of bed, getting dressed or brushing her teeth, though she was pretty sure she'd done all three at some point before she found herself sitting in the cafeteria. The bowl of cereal she'd taken still sat mostly untouched by the time she had to leave for her first class.

Somehow, though, she made it through the rest of

the morning. Everywhere she went, people called out to congratulate her or wish her luck. Dr Starling even mentioned her in assembly that morning. By the time she got to geography class, all she could do was watch the minute hand on the classroom clock march slowly around on its way to eleven forty-five, the time Ms Carmichael had arranged for her to leave class to head over to the shoot location. She'd also arranged for Lani to get out of class so she could come along as moral support.

Finally the time came and the two girls excused themselves. The whole class shouted "Good luck!" as they headed for the door, and Dylan blew Honey a kiss and added, "Break a leg, superstar! Well, not literally. Well, you know what I mean!"

"Ready for this?" Lani asked as she and Honey hurried down the hall, heading for the exit.

"Not even close," Honey replied, her voice shaking.

She'd already dropped off her freshly laundered riding clothes at the barn and polished her tack until it gleamed. Everything else she might need was packed neatly in her equipment bag and waiting for her to load it into the truck. Walker senior Colette Prior, who was widely acknowledged as the best at plaiting manes in the entire school, had volunteered to come down before breakfast and prepare Minnie for her big day, and when Honey arrived and peered into the mare's stall, she saw that the older girl had kept her promise to perfection.

"Go get changed," Lani ordered as she slipped on Minnie's halter. "I'll bring her out and get started on the finishing touches."

"Thanks." Leaving her friend chattering cheerfully to the pony, Honey hurried down the aisle. She grabbed her clothes from the hook in the tack room where she'd left them, then changed in the restroom, slipping a pair of lightweight overalls over her white breeches and black jacket to keep them clean. Then she went back out to help Lani give the already spotless Minnie one last spit-and-polish grooming.

Just as they admitted they couldn't find another speck of dust or stray hair anywhere on the pretty grey pony, Ms Carmichael appeared to check on them. Before long Minnie was in the trailer and the girls were piling into the cab of the truck.

"Here we go," the riding director said, sounding nervous herself as she swung into the driver's seat and consulted the directions.

"Hollywood, here we come!" Lani announced, giving Honey a high five.

The directions led them to a large, luxurious private horse farm with miles of post-and-rail fencing, tall shade trees lining the drive, and a state-of-the-art barn with an enormous attached indoor arena. When they pulled in, right on time, Honey was surprised to see more than a dozen horse trailers and vans lined up in the parking area and a man outside directing traffic. Honey glanced at Ms Carmichael, who looked just as perplexed.

"Hey, what's with all the trailers?" Lani asked.

"I'm not sure." Ms Carmichael carefully manoeuvred the truck into the spot the parking attendant indicated, then cut the engine and yanked on the parking brake. "Let's go find out, shall we?"

"Want me to go investigate while you guys unload?" Lani offered.

Ms Carmichael nodded. "Thanks, Lani. That would be great."

Lani scooted off as Honey and Ms Carmichael hurried around to open the trailer. Minnie was standing inside looking immaculate and tranquil, as if she attended TV shoots every day of the week.

"Let's get her tacked up out here," Ms Carmichael suggested. "That should give Lani time to find out what's going on."

Lani still hadn't returned by the time Minnie's saddle and bridle were on. Honey adjusted the white saddle pad with shaking fingers. "Should I go ahead and get on?" she asked.

Ms Carmichael nodded. "I'll give you a leg up."

Honey felt calmer as soon as she was in the saddle. Giving Minnie a pat, she picked up the reins and rode towards the arena door at a walk with Ms Carmichael beside her.

Lani met them at the door, out of breath and wide-eyed. "You'll never believe this!" she exclaimed.

Honey got a brief glimpse inside. The arena was so large that it contained two separate fenced riding rings with a set of banked seats in between. One was a regulation Olympic-sized dressage ring complete with chains and letters, while the other was smaller and appeared to serve as a warm-up ring. It looked even smaller than it was, since at the moment nearly two dozen formally dressed riders were riding around it, all of them mounted on perfectly groomed, gleaming white ponies!

"Wha – huh?" was all Honey could say.

Lani waved her arms around. "I talked to some assistant guy," she said, keeping her voice low so only Honey and Ms Carmichael could hear. "It turns out they aren't actually shooting the ad today. This is just the audition!"

Ms Carmichael gasped, one hand flying to her mouth. "Oh, no!" she cried, turning to stare at Honey in shock. "We must have misunderstood! I'm so sorry, Honey – I guess I was so pleased by Mr Hutton's compliments on your performance that I didn't ask enough questions."

Honey shook her head, her stomach clenching as the truth sank in. "It's not your fault," she said. "I'm the one who should have asked more questions. My dad even offered to ring Mr Hutton and check on all the details, but I told him not to bother." She bit her lip, glancing towards the warm-up ring, where a flashy pony who appeared to be at least part Andalusian had just performed a flawless piaffe. "But now we know the truth, perhaps we ought to just duck out before anyone sees us."

Lani stared up at her. "What are you talking about?"

Honey felt tears stinging her eyes. "It's hopeless, isn't it?" she said, clutching the reins in her gloved hands. "These people all look like serious full-time dressage riders. I can't hope to compete against the likes of people like that."

"Don't be foolish, Honey," Ms Carmichael said firmly. She appeared to have recovered from her initial surprise. "Mr Hutton thought you and Minnie have what it takes or he wouldn't have invited you to audition."

Lani nodded. "Besides, we're here already," she pointed out. "You might as well give it a shot. What's the worst that could happen?"

"I could die of embarrassment?" Honey offered weakly. But she knew it was no use. Lani and Ms Carmichael were two of the most determined and fearless people she knew, and she was pretty sure they weren't going to let her get away with chickening out.

"You can do this, Honey," Lani said, reaching up and giving her knee a squeeze. "I've always thought you were a way better rider than you give yourself credit for. Dylan and Mal say so, too."

"Really?" Honey quavered.

"Your friends are absolutely right," Ms Carmichael said. "There's no reason to assume you and Minnie are any less competent than any of these others. This will be a great experience for you."

Honey chewed her lower lip as she glanced again at the other riders. With a sinking feeling, she noticed that many of them looked considerably older than she was. Some were clearly brilliant riders mounted on highly trained horses, like the girl on the Andalusian. Others didn't appear quite so skilled in the saddle but looked utterly gorgeous and confident, making Honey wonder if they might be professional models or actors.

She glanced down at herself. Suddenly her nice riding togs and pretty pony felt small and scruffy in comparison.

Ms Carmichael had stepped forward to speak to some other adults clustered near the warm-up ring. At first Honey assumed they were the parents of the other riders, but through their comments she quickly realized they were mostly agents or managers.

"Just as I suspected," she muttered to Lani. "At least half these people are professionals! What am I doing here, anyway?"

"You're here to turn out a fabulous ride just like you did last weekend," Lani told her. "Stop stressing over everybody else and just do your thing. You're going to be great!"

Before they knew it, Ms Carmichael was back and shooing Honey into the warm-up ring. "Just focus on what you're doing," the riding director murmured, pulling out a rag and giving Minnie's muzzle and eyes one last wipe. "Don't worry about the others."

Honey nodded mutely, then rode on through the gate. She paused just inside, waiting for a break in the traffic. A pretty blonde girl of about fifteen was stopped there too, looking perfectly relaxed on the back of a delicate Welsh-type pony with a pearly coat.

"Hi," Honey said to the other girl with an uncertain smile. "Um, are you here for the audition too?"

She realized right away that it was kind of a stupid question. But if the other girl thought so, she didn't let on.

"I sure am," she said, flashing Honey a smile that lit up her face as if a light bulb had just blinked on. "It's a fantastic opportunity, even if it is just a local spot." She shrugged her slender shoulders gracefully. "Besides, I need something to keep me busy – I don't have anything lined up until next month when rehearsals start for a play I'm in up in D.C."

"Oh," Honey said with a gulp. "So, um, you're a professional actor, then?"

The girl nodded matter-of-factly. "Love your accent," she said. "Is it real? I've been working on my British accent lately, but I haven't quite got it down yet." She cleared her throat. "Cheerio, old chap," she said in an exaggerated Cockney trill.

"That sounds good," Honey said politely. "And yes, mine's real. I moved here from England a couple of years ago. I—"

"Genevieve!" one of the well-dressed adults at the rail barked out, interrupting her. "Don't forget, the barn girl warned us that pony gets lazy if he stands around too long. Get out there and make sure he's awake!"

The older girl rolled her eyes at Honey. "Sorry, gotta go," she said. "Good luck, OK?"

"You too," Honey replied, feeling more nervous than ever. Lani and Ms Carmichael could give her all the pep talks they wanted. But how was she supposed to compete against a bunch of professionals?

She did her best to forget about that as she followed Genevieve and her pony out into the throng of other riders. Beginning her warm-up helped her to focus,

92

especially since the crowded ring made her feel as if she were back at Chestnut Hill.

After she and Minnie had been warming up for ten or fifteen minutes, Jim Hutton appeared at the ring and called for attention. "Gather around, please, riders!" he said as he strode towards the centre of the ring.

Honey obeyed along with the others, wondering what came next. She shot a look at Lani and Ms Carmichael, who were watching from the bleachers. Lani tossed her a double thumbs up, while Ms Carmichael waved and smiled. Honey turned her attention back to the director. He began by explaining that the advertisement they were auditioning for was designed to promote the benefits of the Pegasus computer system.

"Our key words are these," he said, holding up one hand to tick the words off on his fingers. "Control. Grace. Elegance. Simplicity. All this will be illustrated by a girl on her white pony. We'll also be using the image of this horse and rider on the packaging and screensavers."

He went on to say that each girl would get the chance to ride to the same piece of music, which the sound people would play a couple of times before they got started. That would give the riders a chance to take it in and decide what type of ride to do.

Then he turned and snapped his fingers at several people bustling around with some complicated-looking equipment on the far end of the stands. "We're not expecting capital-D dressage here," he told the girls. "Just let the music guide you. We're looking for a mood and an image, not any particular movements or anything."

The girl on the Andalusian wrinkled her nose and raised her hand. "But we can ride a real dressage programme if we've prepared one, can't we?" she asked.

Honey shot a panicked look at Lani and Ms Carmichael. She hadn't prepared anything in particular for the audition, since she hadn't known it was an audition in the first place. She'd assumed the director would tell her what to do when she got there.

Never mind, she told herself, taking a deep breath. *I suppose I can just ride the same programme as we did the other day. That's got to be better than nothing, and both Minnie and I are comfortable with it.*

The music started, pouring out of the speakers so loudly that several of the ponies jumped. But Minnie just pricked her ears and blew out through her nostrils in surprise. Honey reached down automatically to give her a pat. But most of her attention was on the music. It was a classical piece, but quite different to the symphony she'd performed to at the All Schools show. This one sounded like a woodwind quartet. Its tone was light and airy, so lively and buoyant that it sounded as if it were being performed by graceful sprites. By the second time through, Honey found herself humming along with the melody.

After that, the director called the first auditioner over to the main ring. Some of the others returned to warming up, but Honey could tell that Minnie was ready and she didn't want to tire her out by warming up for longer than necessary. So she steered the mare over to an out-of-the-way spot to rest as the music began again.

The stands blocked her view of the main ring, so she couldn't watch the first rider. Instead she closed her eyes and sat quietly in the saddle, letting the music wash over and through her. At first she tried to visualize riding her familiar routine to the song. But before long she forgot about that, just picturing herself and Minnie dancing around the ring, directed only by the pace and tone of the music. Each time through, their movements got better and better.

She was so caught up in their imaginary ride that it took her a moment to realize that someone was calling her name. Her eyes flew open.

"Felicity Harper?" a woman with a clipboard was calling from the gate of the warm-up ring. "Is there a Felicity Harper here, please?"

"That's me!" Honey blurted out, nudging Minnie into a trot and heading for the gate. She realized she'd been sitting there through half a dozen audition rides without realizing it. "Sorry. Here I am. I'm Felicity Harper."

The woman nodded and checked something off on her clipboard. "You're on next," she said. "Good luck."

"Thanks." Honey rode out and found Lani there waiting for her, rag in hand.

"You go, girl!" Lani whispered as she hastily wiped off Minnie's face and then Honey's boots. "This is your chance to shine!"

"I hope so," Honey said. The nerves she'd all but forgotten while listening to the music came crowding back, threatening to overwhelm her.

"I *know* so," Lani said confidently. "See, everyone else has been riding to the music. But you and Minnie can go in there and do what you guys do best: *dance* to it!"

9

Honey smiled down at Lani. "Have you been reading my mind?"

"Huh?" Lani looked confused.

"Never mind." Honey looked up. A man was holding the gate open as the previous rider exited. "Here we go."

Giving Minnie a pat, she rode forward. From the moment Honey entered the ring and the music started, she forgot all about the TV commercial and the cameras set up along the rail. Instead she lost herself completely in the music and her pony, letting Minnie dance at walk, trot and canter in flowing shapes around the arena. The little mare obliged, her steps lighter and more graceful than ever, her entire carriage and energy letting Honey know that she was enjoying herself just as much as her rider was.

In fact, Honey was having so much fun that she was almost caught by surprise when the music ended. She brought Minnie to a halt and saluted. Then she glanced uncertainly at the spectators.

Mr Hutton and several of the others applauded briefly. "Nicely done," the director called. "Thank you, Miss Harper." Then he turned away and began muttering busily with the others, while his assistant's voice rang out from the direction of the warm-up ring as she called the next rider.

When she rode out of the ring, Lani was waiting for her. "I'll take Minnie," she said. "That assistant lady said that now they're going to need you to—"

"Come with me please, Miss Harper," a brisk young man called out, racing over and all but dragging Honey out of the saddle. "We'll need to take some test shots next."

Honey barely had time to toss Lani her reins before the young man was ushering her into a side room. Judging by the scents of alfalfa and molasses, Honey guessed that it was some kind of feed room for the adjacent barn. But at the moment it was completely cloaked in black curtains. A tall, narrow woman in jeans and a T-shirt was waiting for her.

"Sit here, please," she ordered as the young man raced off again.

Honey just nodded and did what she was told, feeling confused and a bit intimidated. A second later someone else rolled a large camera forward, so close that Honey leaned back for fear it would run right into her. Then a very bright light blinked on, nearly blinding her and making it impossible to see any of the other people in the room.

"All right, dear," a woman's voice floated out of the

brightness. "I'm going to ask you a few questions. Just answer however you like, OK, sweetheart?"

"Um, sure?" Honey said uncertainly.

The woman began by asking her a few basic questions: her name, her age, how long she'd been riding. Honey answered them all automatically, still feeling flustered and not sure what she was doing there.

"Next question," the woman's voice said. "What do you love most about riding to music?"

Honey didn't stop to think much about that one, either. "I just love to dance," she said passionately.

A chuckle came out from one of the other invisible observers. "Love that British accent!" an unseen man said. "Thanks, honey."

Honey squinted to catch a glimpse of him, wondering how he knew her nickname. As best as she could recall, since arriving at the audition she'd been addressed only by her given name, Felicity.

"All right, darling." The brisk young man had appeared again to shoo her out of the room. "That's all we need from you for right now."

That was when Honey realized the truth. That other man hadn't known her name; it was just a term of endearment. All of these TV people seemed to use those a lot – honey, sweetheart, darling, dear. She guessed it was because they saw too many people at these auditions to bother learning all the names. Feeling rather lost and disoriented, she left the room as the girl she'd met earlier, Genevieve, was whisked past her for her own screen test. The young man deposited her outside to Ms Carmichael, who wrapped her in a big hug.

"Well done, Honey," she said. "You looked amazing out there! I'm so proud of you."

"Thanks," Honey said. "The ride was fun. The rest?" She shot a glance back towards the little room. "Well, I'm not sure what to think about that."

"Never mind. Come on, let's go back to the trailer. Lani's getting Minnie ready to load up." Ms Carmichael steered her gently towards the exit.

Lani glanced up from adjusting the buckles of Minnie's travel sheet as they approached. "There's our superstar!" she crowed, racing over to grab Honey in a big hug. "You guys were totally the best out there today!"

Honey pulled a face. "Hmm, why do I think you'd say that even if I'd fallen off and Minnie had acted like a rodeo bronc?" she quipped weakly. "But that's OK. I realize we haven't got a shot against such impressive competition. We still had fun, though! And Minnie was every bit as fabulous as any of those other ponies." She shot Lani a wink. "Even if she hasn't got her own agent."

"That's the spirit." Ms Carmichael smiled. "Now come on, let's get this unagented pony back home. It's been a long day."

They pulled into the stable yard just before dinner time. Dylan and Malory were at the barn waiting for them, just as Honey had expected. What she hadn't expected was that they weren't alone. Lynsey, Patience, Paris and Jennifer were there, too.

"Uh oh," Honey murmured to Lani as Ms Carmichael manoeuvred into the unloading zone in front of the barn doors. "They're probably all waiting to hear about my fabulous new showbiz career, and now I have to admit it was just an audition."

"What do you mean, *just* an audition?" Lani retorted. "How many of *them* were invited to try out for a real, professional TV commercial alongside a bunch of pro actors?"

Honey couldn't help smiling. "Well, when you put it that way. . ."

As soon as she climbed out of the cab of the truck, Dylan and Malory rushed over. Paris and Jennifer were hot on their heels, though Lynsey and Patience stayed by the barn door as if they were suddenly fascinated with its hinges.

"Well? How was it?" Paris demanded.

"Did Minnie do well? Was she OK being in a strange place?" Malory added.

"Chill, you guys!" Dylan admonished. "Let the poor girl take a breath before you bowl her over with questions." Then she spun to face Honey. "So what did you have to do? Did you have any lines, or was it all riding?"

Lani raised both hands to silence them. "OK, OK!" she exclaimed. "I know you're all dying to hear every little detail."

Lynsey rolled her eyes as she wandered closer

with Patience trotting at her heels. "Think again," she drawled. "I'm just down at the barn checking in on Blue."

"Yeah, right," Dylan said sarcastically. "Like we're supposed to believe you've been 'checking in on Blue' for the past hour."

"Well, actually, she has," Patience piped up. "Some of us have lives of our own, you know, and don't live to hear every little detail about yours."

"Hush," Lani ordered. "Now, we all know Honey is a superstar, and—"

"It was just an audition," Honey blurted out, unable to hold back the truth any longer. "We misunderstood. It wasn't the actual filming after all."

"Really?" Jennifer looked disappointed. "Oh."

Lynsey traded a smug look with Patience. "We should have known," she said. "I mean, how likely is it that someone like you would get discovered just like that?"

Dylan glared at her, then turned back to Honey. "So what happened?" she said. "Don't keep us in suspense. Did you get the part?"

"I don't know," Honey said. "I mean, I doubt it. There were, like, twenty other riders there, and at least half of them were professional actors—"

"But Honey outrode all of them by a mile," Lani broke in. "She was way better than anyone else there."

Malory nodded sympathetically. "I'm sure you both did great. You make a fantastic pair – that's why that director guy noticed you, after all."

"Thanks," Honey said with a smile. "In any case, I'm glad I went. It was a bit nerve-wracking at first, but in the end we had loads of fun."

Just then Ms Carmichael popped her head around the back of the trailer. "Hey," she called. "Is anyone going to help me out here, or am I supposed to unload this pony and feed her bucketloads of carrots all by myself?"

"Coming!" Honey called out, rushing back to help along with her friends.

For the next half hour the four of them treated Minnie like a superstar, plying her with carrots and bits of succulent alfalfa hay while Malory removed her plaits, then rubbed down her legs and left her to enjoy her evening feed. All the other horses and ponies were staying in the barn for the night due to some of the pastures being reseeded, which meant that of course Honey and her friends had to make their way up and down the aisle feeding carrots to every single one.

Finally they made their way up the hill to the cafeteria in time to grab sandwiches before it closed down for the evening. As they all bolted down their overdue dinners, Honey's mobile buzzed in her pocket. She pulled it out and saw that she had a text from Josh.

"Oh," she said, scanning it. "I forgot that he knew about this, too. I'd better text him back and let him know it was just an audition. I'll need to let my family know, as well."

Her fingers flew over the tiny keyboard, filling Josh in on the basics. He texted back almost immediately. Honey laughed out loud when she read his message.

"What?" Dylan demanded, picking a bit of tomato out of her sandwich.

"It's Josh again," Honey said, holding out her phone so the others could see. "He says that if he were the director, he'd definitely choose me and Minnie."

Lani leaned over to read the message and laughed too. "Especially if you were auditioning for *Annie Get Your Gun*," she read. "Hey, that's a thought! Now that you've mastered dressage to music, maybe the next step is a dressage *musical*!"

"Ooh, I like!" Dylan sat up straight. "Instead of the auditorium, we could hold the show in the indoor ring. All the actors could ride instead of walk, and the dance numbers could be an all-dressage revue. . ."

By now Malory was giggling wildly. "I love it!" she cried. "But only if Honey plays the lead."

"Of course!" Dylan exclaimed. "Who else would fit the role but our own dressage superstar?"

Honey grinned. "I'm in," she said. "But only if I don't have to audition!"

"Mum? It's me," Honey said into the phone a little while later. The girls had returned to Adams House after their meal. Dylan, Malory and Lani had already headed to the common room to hang out, but Honey had stopped off in her room for a bit of privacy while she called her family. She'd already talked to Sam, who was disappointed on her behalf but supportive. Next she'd dialled her parents' house.

"Oh, hello, sweetheart." Her mother sounded distracted. "We just walked in. How are you?"

"Fine. I just wanted to let you and Dad know about the filming today," Honey said. "Except the thing is, it wasn't exactly a filming, more of an audition for the filming. . ."

"Mmm? Oh, you mean the TV riding commercial?" her mother said. "What was that about an audition?"

Honey explained the situation once again. "As it turned out, I was just one of at least twenty people trying out for the part," she finished. "So I wouldn't be looking for me on TV anytime soon."

"Well, never mind," her mother said. "The important thing is you did your best, hmm?"

"Right. Is Dad around? I wanted to tell him, too."

"I'm afraid he's tied up at the moment," her mother replied. "And I hate to say it, but I'd better hang up. Can we talk more about this in a day or two?"

"Of course. Bye, Mum."

Honey hung up the phone, humming a bit of the song she'd ridden to that day. Her mind wandered back to her ride, making her smile. Even if her brush with fame hadn't turned out quite as expected, she was grateful for the extra time with Minnie.

So what if I'm not going to be a TV star? she thought. *I don't need fame and fortune to be happy, after all. My life's pretty perfect just as it is!*

10

"Three X minus two equals . . . drat!" Honey muttered.

Lani leaned over from the next seat in the cafeteria. "Sure you don't want my help?" she asked through a mouthful of oatmeal. It was Friday morning and the four friends were at breakfast.

Honey looked up and blew a strand of hair out of her eyes. "Thanks for the offer," she said. "But it won't do me any good for you to solve the problems for me if I don't understand how to do it myself. Especially if Mrs O'Hara decides to give us one of her infamous Friday quizzes today."

Dylan was blinking sleepily over her second blueberry smoothie. "I don't see why we have to study algebra anyway," she mumbled with a yawn. "It's not like we're ever going to need to figure out the value of X or whatever in our everyday life. At least I'm pretty sure *I'm* not."

Honey tended to agree with that sentiment, though she knew it wouldn't do her any good if there did turn out to be a quiz that day in class. "It's all my own fault, anyway," she said with a sigh. "I was so busy thinking about that silly TV commercial in class on Tuesday that I didn't pay any attention at all to the lesson."

"We might not have a quiz today," Malory said optimistically. "At least, I hope not. I'm not sure I understood this week's homework too well myself."

"No wonder." Honey stared at the textbook spread out beside her plate, the numbers and symbols seeming to dance around meaninglessly on the page. "As far as I'm concerned, algebra might as well be a different language."

Dylan yawned again. "A stupid, boring language," she said. "Learning Swahili or something would be more useful."

"Oh, come on," Lani protested. "It's not *that* bad."

"Easy for you to say," Dylan countered. "We can't all be math geniuses."

Honey was about to agree when she spotted Ms Carmichael entering the cafeteria. "Hey, what's she doing here?" she commented in surprise. The riding director always looked a little out of place anywhere but in the stable yard. Honey guessed it would be the same if she saw, say, Dr Duffy or Mme Dubois wandering down the barn aisle.

"You didn't forget to turn off the water hydrant again when you filled buckets last night, did you?" Malory asked Dylan.

"I don't think so." Dylan sat up a little straighter, peering across the crowded cafeteria at her aunt. "Anyway, she doesn't look mad, so that's probably not it."

Just then Ms Carmichael spotted them and waved. "There you are," she greeted them, her eyes sparkling. "Sorry to disturb your breakfast, but this news is way too big to wait until riding class!"

"What is it?" Lani asked curiously.

Ms Carmichael looked at Honey. "I just got a call from Jim Hutton."

"Who?" Dylan asked. Then her eyes widened, making her look a lot less sleepy all of a sudden. "Wait, you mean that director dude?"

Ms Carmichael nodded. "Honey, you and Minnie got the part!" she cried. "He wants you to be in the commercial!"

Honey gasped, hardly daring to believe her ears. "Really?" she cried. "Minnie and I are going to be on TV after all?"

"Whoo hoo!" Dylan was fully awake now. She leaped to her feet, nearly knocking over her cereal bowl as she pumped both fists in the air. "You did it, Honey!"

Lani was on her feet, too. "I knew it!" she crowed. "I told you guys Honey and Minnie were the best! Didn't I tell you?"

"You told us!" Dylan cried, grabbing Lani and spinning her around. Soon the two of them were doing an impromptu jig in the middle of the cafeteria.

Malory laughed. "Congratulations, Honey," she said, leaning over to give her a hug. "This is great!"

By now everyone at the adjoining tables had turned to see what the commotion was about.

"What's going on over there?" Rosie Williams called

from the table where she was sitting with a group of other seniors.

"Honey got the part!" Dylan shouted at the top of her lungs.

"Hush!" Honey felt herself blush, but at the same time she couldn't stop grinning. She watched as Dylan raced over to fill in the older girls on the whole story.

The news spread like wildfire. Soon everyone in the cafeteria was cheering and calling out their congratulations. Even the kitchen staff came out from behind the counter and gave Honey a standing ovation.

Lani grinned. "See?" she whispered to Honey. "I said all along that you were a superstar!"

"Did you reach your parents?" Lani asked as Honey slid into the seat beside her in their history classroom seconds before the late bell.

Honey nodded, too out of breath after running all the way from the student centre to answer for a moment. "They're thrilled," she gasped out at last. "They want to take me and Sam out for dinner tonight to celebrate."

"Sweet!" Lani grinned.

"I wanted you to come, too," Honey went on. "I thought you should help us celebrate, since you were such a great help at the auditions and everything." She shrugged apologetically. "But Mum said this time she thought it should just be a family occasion."

"That's OK. They probably want you all to themselves so they can spend the whole time telling

109

you how great you are," Lani said cheerfully as Mrs Von Beyer hurried into the room and called for attention.

Honey sat back in her seat, her mind wandering as the teacher started writing the day's lesson on the board. It was still hard to believe this was really happening – and happening so fast! The shoot would take place on Saturday, a week from the following day. Ms Carmichael had told Honey that the production team would be emailing her that afternoon with a list of the movements she and Minnie would be expected to perform. The riding director had promised to set up an extra practice session with Mr Musgrave as soon as possible so Honey could start learning them.

I hope I can do this, Honey thought with a shiver. Then an image of Minnie came into her mind, and she remembered how wonderful it had felt to ride the little mare as she danced to the music. That made her smile. *I'm not on my own*, she told herself. *I know we can definitely do this!*

"Hurry up," Dylan called down the barn aisle. "You know old Musgrave doesn't like it when you're late."

"He also doesn't like it when you call him 'old Musgrave'," a dry voice came from the far end of the aisle.

Honey glanced up from tightening Minnie's girth and saw Mr Musgrave standing just inside the doors, giving Dylan a withering look. She lowered her head to hide her smile as Dylan stammered out an apology.

"Good luck, Honey," Malory whispered, rushing past and giving Minnie a quick pat.

"Thanks." Honey grabbed Minnie's bridle off a hook nearby as the dressage coach approached. "Thank you for agreeing to help me with this, Mr Musgrave," she said.

"It's my pleasure, Miss Harper." Mr Musgrave was holding a piece of paper. He glanced down at it. "Ms Carmichael gave me the list of movements the producers sent over. It all looks fairly straightforward – no flying changes or anything else we haven't worked on in our regular lessons."

"Good," Honey said with relief. She'd spent at least half of French class worrying that she'd walk into the shoot next weekend to find that Mr Hutton expected her to start performing piaffe and passage!

"However, we'll want to work on some transitions and schooling figures," Mr Musgrave went on. "It sounds as if you'll need to be very precise with those sorts of elements, similar to a real dressage test."

Honey nodded. Judging by the tone of his voice and the look on his face, she had the distinct feeling that to Mr Musgrave, dancing to music definitely did *not* qualify as "real" dressage!

"Go ahead and put the bridle on," the coach added, glancing at Minnie. "I'll meet you in the indoor arena in five minutes."

"OK," Honey said.

As Mr Musgrave strode off, Honey's friends scurried forward to help unclip Minnie from the cross-ties and slip her bridle on. "Whew!" Dylan whispered with a nervous glance over her shoulder. "That was embarrassing. Let's hope he forgets I called him old before our next dressage lesson, or he'll probably make me ride the whole thing without stirrups."

"Or maybe he'll make you sit backwards in the saddle," Malory suggested.

Dylan's eyes widened with interest. "Hey, that could be kind of fun," she mused, shooting a thoughtful look at Morello, who had his head hanging out over his stall door watching them. "I might have to try that sometime. . ."

"Are you guys going to stay and watch?" Honey asked, too anxious to join in with Dylan's comedy plans.

Lani grinned. "Try and stop us!"

They all followed Honey and Minnie into the indoor arena, then scooted off to find seats in the viewing stands. Honey led Minnie over to the mounting block, adjusted her stirrups, and climbed on. For the next forty-five minutes, she barely had time to think, let alone check on her friends. Mr Musgrave kept her busy polishing her dressage skills and practising everything she'd need to do at the shoot. They didn't rehearse the entire sequence of movements in order, but the coach helped her figure out how to put it all together by riding it in smaller chunks, sometimes to the music and sometimes not.

"Very nice," the instructor said with a nod after Honey and Minnie executed a tidy leg yield at trot.

Honey smiled her thanks. Mr Musgrave tended to be stingy with praise, so it meant a lot to hear him say anything nice about her riding at all.

He seems to think we can do this, she thought, bending forward to give Minnie a pat as she awaited her next instructions. *So do my friends, my family, and Ms Carmichael. Who am I to argue?*

"Quit wriggling around," Dylan ordered.

"I can't help it." Honey sneaked another peek at her watch. "I'm just trying to keep an eye on the time."

Her three best friends were in her dorm room helping her get ready for the celebratory dinner with her family. Dylan and Lani had insisted that she should wear the same outfit she'd worn to Lani's science ceremony, and Honey had been happy to agree. She was already dressed in the cute red dress and bolero jacket, and now Dylan was carefully applying some finishing touches to her make-up.

"Does my hair look all right?" Honey asked as Dylan turned away to look for something in the make-up bag she'd brought with her.

"Fantastic," Malory assured her.

Lani nodded. "Like a superstar."

Honey rolled her eyes and smiled. "You know, if you keep calling me that, I might start to believe it," she quipped. "Then what will you do? You'll have a friend with a massively swollen head."

"That's OK," Lani said. "Superstars are allowed to have big heads. It's part of the job."

There was a buzz. "Oops, I think that's my phone," Honey said. She ducked away as Dylan came at her with a lash curler. Hurrying over to her bed, she dug around

113

in the piles of clothes, hairbrushes and make-up until she found her mobile.

"Is it your folks?" Lani asked.

Honey shook her head as she checked the message. "It's a text from Josh," she said.

"Honey and Josh, sittin' in a tree!" Dylan began in a sing-song. "Is he texting to congratulate you on your fabulous new life of stardom?"

"Actually, yes." Honey bit her lip, realizing that in the whirlwind of excitement that day, she'd completely forgotten to fill him in on landing the commercial role. "Sam must have told him about it," she said as she scanned his message. "I'd better write back and apologize for not letting him know myself."

She perched on the edge of the bed and did so. Within seconds she received another text in response.

"What's he say?" Lani asked.

Honey read the new text, then glanced up with a smile. "He understands," she said with relief. "And, um. . ."

"What?" Dylan demanded. "Is there something more? Something adorable and romantic, perhaps?"

Malory snorted. "Settle down, gossip girl."

"It's OK." Honey ducked her head so her friends wouldn't see her blush. "He says he'll help me celebrate by treating me to one of those Hershey's Kiss milkshakes next time we're all in town."

"Aww!" Dylan grinned. "Sounds like a date!"

"Speaking of which, don't forget you still have a date tonight with your family," Malory reminded Honey, glancing at her watch. "It's almost seven."

Five minutes later Honey was fully dressed and made up and waiting in the lobby. At seven o'clock on the dot, she spotted headlights flashing as a car turned into the Adams drive. Seconds later her parents' familiar silver saloon pulled up outside the lobby doors.

"There they are," she told the evening monitor, a kind-faced older woman who also worked part-time in the cafeteria. "I should be back in a few hours."

"Have a nice time, dear," the monitor replied, scribbling Honey's name and the time on her sign-out sheet before returning to the mystery novel she was reading.

Honey ducked out into the chilly evening air. The car door swung open when she was halfway to it.

"There she is, ladies and gentlemen!" her brother's voice sang out from inside. "Please welcome megastar Felicity 'Honey' Harper. No autographs, please!" He leaned over and snapped a few photos with his mobile.

Honey blinked as the tiny flash lit up in her face. "Get lost," she joked, shoving Sam back inside and then climbing in beside him. Her father was glancing back from the driver's seat, with her mother sitting beside him.

"Hello, Honey," he said. "Buckle up and we'll get on the road."

Honey snapped on her seatbelt. "Where are we going for dinner?"

"We thought we might try Verdi's," her mother replied. "Does that sound all right?"

"Sure, I love that place." Honey couldn't help smiling

ruefully as she thought of the last time she'd been to that particular Italian restaurant. She and her friends had been trying to set up Malory's father with Matilda Harvey from the craft shop, not knowing that he was already secretly dating Ms Carmichael.

It's amazing all the odd situations I find myself in these days, thanks to my friends, she thought. *Still, I wouldn't trade it for the world!*

"What are you grinning about?" Sam demanded, leaning over to poke her in the arm.

"Nothing," Honey said, settling back against the seat. "Just feeling happy, that's all."

"It's wonderful hearing all about your riding adventures," Mrs Harper said when Honey paused for breath while describing how well Minnie had done in their dressage practice earlier. "But perhaps you'd better eat before your food gets cold."

"Oops." Honey looked down at her mostly untouched plate of pasta and realized her mother was right. She'd been so busy telling her family about everything that had happened that she'd hardly had a chance to eat a thing. She picked up her fork and twirled some linguini on to it. Verdi's was crowded with other diners, but Honey and her family were seated at a quiet booth along one wall. The tall backs of the built-in booths cut down on the noise from the other tables, making those seats much quieter than those in the centre part of the candlelit, pink-and-cream restaurant.

Of course, it's not nearly as romantic over here as it was at the table we booked for Mr O'Neil and Matilda, she thought, glancing at a recessed alcove nearby, where a young couple were drinking wine and staring into each other's eyes at their table for two. *Or as romantic as we'd intended it to be, anyway. How were we to know that Matilda already had a boyfriend. . .?*

She was so lost in the memory – embarrassing at the time, but amusing in hindsight – that it took her a moment to realize her father had just raised his wine glass. "Shall we have a toast?" he asked.

"Let's do." Mrs Harper picked up her wine glass as well.

Honey grabbed her glass of iced tea and held it up, while Sam lifted his soft drink. "What are we toasting?" Sam asked.

"To Honey – and new beginnings," his father said.

Sam smirked. "You mean the beginning of Honey being a movie star?"

Smiling, Mr Harper shook his head and traded a look with his wife. "No, not that new beginning," he said. "Well, yes, that one too, of course. But we also have a different new beginning to celebrate."

Honey's arm was getting tired, so she lowered her glass and took a sip. "What do you mean?" she asked, picking up her fork and poking at her pasta.

Her father's smile grew broader. "We wanted to tell you both in person," he said. "It's such a wonderful surprise. You see, I've been offered a full professorship!"

Honey gasped. Her father was a lecturer at the University of Virginia, and she knew it had always been his plan to make professor one day. "Oh, Dad!" she cried. "That's so fantastic! When do you start?"

"In May," Mrs Harper answered for him. "It won't give us much time, but they're eager for your father to begin as soon as possible."

Sam shrugged. "Yeah, it doesn't give us that long to pull together a proper professor party," he agreed. "But hey, we can do it."

"That's not quite what I meant." Mrs Harper hesitated, glancing at her husband.

Mr Harper nodded. "You see, kids, the thing is, the professorship's in Oxford," he explained.

"You mean it's not at UVA?" Honey blinked. "Or wait, do you mean it's at a satellite campus? Is there an Oxford, Virginia?"

Her parents traded another look. "No, I'm talking about Oxford, England," Mr Harper said. "We're going home!"

11

Honey's fork clattered against her plate as she stared at her father in horror. "What?" she blurted out.

"Are you serious?" Sam exclaimed, sounding equally stunned. "We're moving back to England?"

Mrs Harper nodded. "I know this must come as a surprise," she said. "But just think, we'll be back near the rest of the family again!"

Honey couldn't speak. She could feel fury building inside her – a very uncharacteristic feeling for her. "No!" she cried, unable to hold it inside her. She shoved her plate away and stared wild-eyed at her parents. "You can't do this!"

"Honey, please—" her father began.

She shook her head so hard that she dislodged the hair grips holding the upsweep Dylan had crafted so carefully. "You can't!" she insisted. "It isn't fair. I've had a perfect day today, and now you have to go and ruin it!"

Her parents traded an anxious look. "Please let's not be childish about this, Honey," Mrs Harper said. "Your father's job—"

"Right. It's Dad's job, so of course we all have to up and move again. Everybody else's wishes always come ahead of mine!" Honey clenched her fists around handfuls of the ivory tablecloth, nearly tipping over her glass. "First it was Sam, now it's you." She glared at her father. "What about me? What about what I want? Don't I matter at all in this family?"

"Of course you matter." Her father reached across the table to touch her gently on the back of her hand. She recoiled at his touch as if she'd been burned, shoving both hands beneath the table into her lap.

"I thought you two would be pleased at the thought of going home." Mrs Harper gazed pleadingly at Honey. "You can go back to your old school, see all your old friends – perhaps we might even be able to find your pony Rocky and buy him back. Wouldn't that be lovely?"

"No!" Honey's eyes widened in dismay as she recognized just what all this would mean. "I don't want Rocky back! Minnie is the only pony I care about, and she's right here in Virginia. This is my home now! Not England!"

Her mother bit her lip, looking distressed. Meanwhile Sam shot Honey a warning look.

Honey saw it and felt her heart sink even further. Glancing at her parents, she saw the expressions on their faces and realized she'd gone too far. She stared wordlessly down at her half-eaten dinner.

After a long, awkward moment of silence, her father cleared his throat. "Perhaps we'd better get the bill," he said quietly, signalling for the waiter. "I suspect none of us is in the mood for dessert."

A few minutes later they left the restaurant and walked to the car. Sam asked their father a few questions about the professorship, but Honey hardly heard them. Her mind was churning and the little bit of pasta she'd eaten before her father's bombshell sat heavily in her stomach. She could tell her parents were disappointed by the way she'd reacted, and part of her regretted shouting out in the restaurant. But it was too late to take the words back now.

Besides, why should I take them back? she thought bleakly, glancing around at the quaint shops, tidy homes, and pleasant, lamplit streets of Cheney Falls. Her home. *I meant everything I said.*

After checking in with the monitor in the dorm lobby, Honey headed upstairs. She could hear the usual cheerful after-dinner commotion coming from the common room. As she neared the door, the distinctive sound of Lani's laugh drifted out. Dylan gleefully shouted out something about Malory and Malory retorted in kind, resulting in general hilarity.

Honey winced, not ready to face her friends at the moment. The car ride home had passed mostly in silence except for a few attempts by Sam to break the ice. That had given Honey plenty of time to think about exactly what this move would mean – leaving Chestnut Hill, saying goodbye to her teachers, her favourite pony, and most of all the best friends she'd ever had in her life. How was she ever going to tell them?

She tiptoed past the common room door as quickly as she could, then hurried straight to her room. When she opened the door, the lights were on. The place was deserted, but there was a huge banner hung from the curtain rod reading *Congratulations, Honey – Our Superstar!* with tons of sparkly star cut-outs dancing across it. Balloons were everywhere, all of them various shades of blue, from pale cornflower to navy. Honey's eyes filled with tears as she realized her friends must have chosen them especially for her because they knew that blue was her favourite colour.

Brushing a few stray balloons off her bed, she flopped down on her duvet and let the tears come. Soon she was sobbing so loudly that she was afraid they'd hear her all the way down in the common room. She got up, changed quickly into her pyjamas and crawled under the covers to muffle the sound. Burying her face in her pillow, she cried until she couldn't cry any more. After that, she just lay there trying not to think.

When Lani burst in an hour later, Honey tensed but didn't move. She still had her face in her pillow, so she hoped her room-mate would assume she was asleep. Indeed, she heard Lani breathe out an "Oops!" and then start tiptoeing around getting ready for bed.

Before long the room's lights snapped off, and a few minutes later came the slow, rhythmic sound of Lani's breathing as she dropped off to sleep. Only then did Honey dare move, carefully turning over on to her back. But she lay awake for a long time after that, doing nothing but stare at the shadows of the trees outside swaying across the pale ceiling.

At some point during the night Honey finally dropped off. She awoke with a start when someone's alarm went off faintly in the room next door, and opened her eyes to see the room filled with bright morning sunshine. For a moment she couldn't remember why her eyes felt so crusty and tired and her insides hollow from crying. Why had she been so upset?

Then it all came back in a rush. Her father's new job. Moving back to England. Leaving Chestnut Hill. The desolate, betrayed feeling returned stronger than ever.

She heard Lani stir in the bed on the other side of the room. Squeezing her eyes shut, Honey reached a decision then and there. She wouldn't tell her friends. Not yet. Why ruin their day the way her parents had ruined hers? They were all so excited about the TV commercial – at least maybe this way they could all enjoy it without a massive shadow hanging over everything. Not to mention the school spirit collage, Dylan's latest scheme to ride Morello backwards, their next movie night in the common room. . .

Honey felt tears threatening again as she thought of everything she'd be missing. But she did her best to hold them back. Lani would notice if she looked too miserable, and then the game would be up.

She waited until Lani crawled out of bed and

stumbled off to the bathroom. Then she quickly sat up and rubbed at her face with her bed sheet, hoping her eyes weren't too red from last night. She was sitting at her desk brushing her hair when her room-mate returned, hair wet and wrapped in a robe.

"Oh good, you're up!" Lani greeted her. "Have fun at dinner last night?" She grinned. "I'm guessing you must've had two helpings of Verdi's famous tiramisu – that would explain why you were out like a light when I got back here."

Honey forced a chuckle. "No, I'm afraid there was no room for dessert," she said. "It was a long day, that's all."

"True. Musgrave worked you and Minnie pretty hard." Lani yawned and turned away, digging through her underwear drawer. "But it'll be worth it when you blow everyone away at the shoot next week, right? Oh! By the way, how thrilled were your parents and Sam when you told them all the details?"

"Pretty thrilled," Honey said with as much cheerfulness as she could muster. It wasn't easy, since she'd just realized that Lani would be hit doubly hard whenever she did find out about this. Not only would she be losing a best friend in Honey, but her budding relationship with Sam as well.

It's not fair, Honey thought bleakly. *Why does this have to happen just when everything is so perfect?*

"Brrr!" Malory cried, blowing out her breath in a little puff. "I thought it was supposed to be spring!"

Dylan laughed as Morello spooked at a blowing leaf.

"I know," she said. "This wind and the cool temperatures are making the ponies pretty skittish!"

Lani urged Colorado forward as he stopped and tried to dive for a patch of new grass poking up at the base of an oak. "Come on, let's canter as soon as we get out in the open," she suggested. "Otherwise we'll be late to meet the boys."

"Why do you care?" Dylan asked. "I thought Sam called this morning to say he wasn't coming. Isn't that right, Honey?"

Honey smiled weakly, feeling sorry that her brother had taken ill but selfishly glad that he wouldn't be able to spill their terrible secret. "Yes, he came down with a cold overnight," she said. "He still wanted to meet us, but my parents wouldn't hear of him coming along and infecting us all. Besides, they're still pretty protective of him – they make him stay in bed if he gets so much as a sniffle."

Dylan steered Morello around a spot of half-frozen mud. "He'd probably have to come down with the bubonic plague to get any attention from your parents these days," she said with a wicked smile. "It can't be easy having a sister who's on the verge of becoming an international superstar."

"Stop it," Malory chided, shooting Honey an anxious look. "It's a little too soon to joke about Sam being sick after he just got well again."

"No, it's all right. I'm sure if Sam were here he'd be making the same sort of comments himself." Honey forced herself to laugh. So far, pretending nothing was wrong was turning out to be harder than she'd expected. She'd noticed Lani shooting her a few odd looks as they had breakfast and then went on their usual Saturday-morning trail ride. And now Malory seemed to be noticing she wasn't herself as well.

"Here's our canter spot," Dylan announced as they left the shelter of the trees and emerged at the edge of a broad meadow. "Last one back to the barn has to clean my tack!"

Honey clucked to Minnie as the other three ponies took off. She was a bit alarmed to see Colorado duck his head and kick out in a mini buck, though Lani just laughed and urged him on faster. Tybalt had his head straight up in the air at first, but when he realized Malory was letting him go, he surged forward, quickly passing Morello, though Malory was careful to keep him behind Colorado as the speedy buckskin took the lead. Minnie wasn't as fast as the other three but she galloped on gamely, one ear pricked forward to track the other horses while the other stayed cocked back towards her rider.

They were moving fast enough that the cool wind brought tears to Honey's eyes. She did her best to blink them away and not get distracted by wondering exactly how many more times she might get to canter across this meadow. If this was going to be one of her last trail rides with her friends, she didn't want to waste a moment of it feeling sorry for herself.

By the time Honey and her friends climbed on board, the Chestnut Hill minibus was already crowded with students planning to spend the afternoon in Cheney Falls. "Hey, you guys!" Rosie Williams called, waving as the girls looked around for seats. "How are things going with your school collage?"

"You heard about that, huh?" Dylan called back, puffing up a bit with pride. Rosie was not only a senior, but one of the most popular girls in school. "It's coming along." She shot a glance at Honey. "Er, isn't it?"

Honey nodded. "I've been a little distracted this week," she told Rosie. "But we're hoping it will be finished in time to make the cover of the next issue of *View From the Hill*."

"Cool," Rosie said. "Let me know if I can do anything to help."

"All aboard that's coming aboard?" the driver called out as he shut the doors. "Next stop, Cheney Falls!"

His passengers were a cheerful bunch, spending much of the short ride into town singing every school song they could think of. Honey tried to join in, but found herself distracted by gazing out the window at the familiar sights sliding past. There were the tall wrought-iron school gates, grand and timeless with their Latin crest and ornate tree motif. How many more times would she pass through them? Then she spotted the gnarled old maple at the end of the road that was just budding in spring green. Would she ever again see it turn its autumn shades of vivid scarlet and orange? Next came the sign for the turn-off to Closer Road, which was forever getting its C stolen so it spelled out Loser Road instead. . .

When the minibus pulled to the curb on Main Street, Dylan leaned across Honey to peer out the window. "There they are!" she said, waving at Josh and Caleb, who were waiting outside the coffee shop with their hands shoved into their coat pockets against the chill.

"Hi! Where do you want to go first?" Josh asked, rushing over to meet Honey as she disembarked. "Should we go get that milkshake to celebrate your big news?"

Honey flinched. "But how did you—" she blurted out before catching herself. For a second she'd thought he was talking about her move back to the UK. But his expression was happy and excited, and she realized he was referring to the TV commercial.

I suppose it's lucky Sam hasn't told them yet, she thought. Even though her brother didn't live at school, she couldn't have blamed him for wanting to call his friends and share such massive news.

"Milkshake?" Dylan wrinkled her nose as she hopped out of the bus in time to hear Josh's comment. "We only had breakfast an hour ago. Let's do some shopping first."

Caleb grinned. "Is that all you think about? Shopping?"

"Yep, pretty much," Malory said as she joined them on the pavement. "Dylan lives for shopping. And horses, of course."

"Don't forget scheming and making trouble." Lani was the last one out. "She definitely lives for that, too."

128

Dylan rolled her eyes. "Whatever," she pronounced. "Anyway, Josh, I know you're all psyched that your girlfriend's practically a movie star. But the milkshake will have to wait. I'm dying to pick up the latest CD by Katy Perry."

"CD?" Lani echoed in surprise. "Why don't you just download it on to your iPod?"

Dylan looked sheepish. "I can't," she admitted. "At least not for another week. Mme Dubois confiscated it when she caught me sneaking a listen during language lab the other day."

Malory laughed. "Why am I not surprised?"

"I wouldn't mind stopping at the music store myself," Honey put in. Dylan's words had reminded her of an errand that had seemed terribly important yesterday afternoon, though now that seemed like an eternity ago. "The song Minnie and I will be dancing to in that commercial isn't on iTunes and I want to get my own copy if I can find it. That way I can listen to it while I'm walking around school this week."

"OK," Josh said, smiling at her. "Music store it is!"

"Let me see it again." Dylan turned around and kneeled on the seat in the minibus she was sharing with Malory, allowing her to peer back into the seat behind her, where Honey was sitting beside Lani.

"See what?" Lani asked innocently.

Malory popped up beside Dylan and laughed. "Don't tease her," she said. "She's just overwhelmed with Josh's romanticness."

"Is romanticness a word?" Lani wondered aloud.

"If it's not, it should be." Dylan raised an eyebrow at Honey. "Now come on, let's see it!"

Honey smiled, blushing slightly as she fished a delicate necklace out from beneath the collar of her jacket. "I still can't believe he gave me this," she murmured, tilting her head to one side to get a look at the pendant, which was in the shape of a dancing horse.

After stopping at the music store, the whole group had spent another hour or two wandering around town together before heading over to the Dairy Den. That was when Josh had finally bought Honey that milkshake – and pulled out a small, wrapped box.

"I got this for you," he'd said shyly.

The two of them were the only ones from their group still in line waiting for the employees to finish making their shakes, which gave them a tiny bit of privacy for the first time all day. Honey had opened the box and found the dancing horse necklace nestled inside on a bed of blue satin.

"Oh!" she'd cried as soon as she saw it. "It's gorgeous!"

"Do you really like it?" Josh had grinned self-consciously, leaning a little closer. "I mean, it made me think of you as soon as I saw it, but if it's not something you'd wear or whatever. . ."

"No, I love it." Honey had leaned over then, impulsively giving him a quick kiss on the cheek. "Thank you."

Josh had blushed deep crimson. "Here, let me put it on you," he'd blurted out, fumbling for the box.

Thinking back on it all now, Honey smiled, a little amazed by her own forwardness. "By the way, Dylan," she said as her friend cooed over the pendant. "Thanks for not breaking into that 'sitting in a tree' song of yours when you saw me kiss Josh."

Dylan widened her eyes, the picture of innocence. "Whatever do you mean?" she said. "I didn't see a thing."

"Get real, Walsh." Lani rolled her eyes. "When it comes to kissing or anything romantic, you've got, like, built-in radar."

Dylan shrugged. "What can I say? I love love." She leaned both arms on the back of the seat and smiled. "In any case, Honey, all I can say is it's a good thing you're such an awesome person."

"What do you mean?" Malory asked her.

"Think about it," Dylan replied. "Honey's got everything. A cute boyfriend who buys her cool presents, a gorgeous pony to ride –"

"Thanks mostly to you," Honey broke in.

"– a starring role in a TV commercial," Dylan went on without responding to that. "The best friends in the world. . ."

"Well, that part's true," Lani agreed with a nod. "You really are pretty lucky, Honey. Then again, we all are. After all, we get to be friends with you!"

She reached over and gave Honey a quick hug. Honey smiled and kept herself busy tucking her pendant back under the jacket so it wouldn't get caught on the zipper. Her friends were right. She had the perfect life. How could she tell them her parents were planning on taking it all away?

12

It was a strange week at school. Honey spent most of it worrying that someone was going to find out the truth. She'd called Sam and begged him not to tell his friends until she was ready, and he'd reluctantly agreed to wait at least until he returned to school.

"Mum and Dad are freaking out about this stupid cold," he'd said, sounding cranky. "They're threatening to keep me home for the entire week."

Honey had smiled wistfully at that. "'Freaking out', eh?" she'd echoed. "My, but you're sounding like a real American, aren't you?"

Sam had just sighed. "Oh, Honey. . . Listen, I hear Dad coming in. I'd better go."

She'd spoken to him another time or two since. But the conversations had been brief and kind of awkward. Her chats with her parents had been even worse, though it was obvious that they were trying to be extra nice to her.

But what good does that do? Honey thought miserably as her mother chattered on during a call on Wednesday evening, telling her how excited all their relatives back in the UK were about Honey's TV commercial. *They're still ruining my life.*

"What was that?" she blurted out, realizing that while her mind was drifting, her mother had asked her a question.

"I said, do you need anything from home before your shoot?" Mrs Harper repeated patiently. "Spare clothes, anything at all? I could run it over to Chestnut Hill tomorrow afternoon or the day after."

"No, it's OK," Honey replied. "I have everything I need here."

"All right, then," her mother said. "We'll be on location Saturday to cheer you on and watch you shoot the advert."

"Whatever," Honey said dully.

Her mother paused, then cleared her throat. "All right, love," she said. "I'd better go. Talk to you later."

"Sure, Mum. Bye." Honey felt guilty as she hung up. She still felt terrible about causing a scene in the restaurant, and she hated the way she'd been acting towards her parents ever since. But she couldn't help it. It was difficult enough mustering up the energy to fake being normal in front of her friends and everyone else at school. She just didn't have enough left over to do so for her family, too.

All she could do to distract herself from feeling wretched was do her best to keep busy so she wouldn't have time to think. Her teachers seemed ready to cooperate with that plan by assigning a virtual deluge of homework. Between that and her daily dressage practices, Honey didn't even have time to work on the collage, though occasionally one of the other members of the Get Crafty club would mention something to her about it.

I'll have to focus on the collage as soon as the shoot is over so we get it finished on time, she thought after listening to Razina describe some early spring wild flowers she'd found in the woods that she wanted to press and add to it. *At least that way I can take a picture of it to help me remember Chestnut Hill for ever.*

"Careful!" Lani darted forward and stuck a napkin under Honey's chin, almost tripping over a bucket someone had left in the stable aisle.

Honey finished taking a bite of the muffin she'd grabbed from the dorm vending machine. "I'm all right," she mumbled through the mouthful. "I got the plain rather than the blueberry in case of stains, remember? Besides, they said they'd have an outfit for me to wear when I get there. So it probably wouldn't matter if I dribbled my entire breakfast down my front."

Honey shivered. The day of the shoot had finally arrived. The excitement of the occasion had even chased away most of the lurking gloom that had haunted her all week, at least for a couple of hours, and she felt genuinely excited – not to mention nervous! She glanced down the aisle. Minnie was standing placidly in

135

a set of cross-ties while Malory and Dylan fussed over her. The mare's coat gleamed and her tail was like a silken white waterfall.

The roar of an engine came from just outside. "Sounds like our ride's here," Dylan said. She patted Minnie on the neck. "Or rather, *your* ride, Min-min."

"Can you guys carry my gear out and see if they're ready to load Minnie?" Honey asked. "I'll put her sheet and boots on. If you don't mind, I'd like a moment with her on my own."

Malory smiled understandingly. "Sure," she said. "Come on, you guys."

They hurried off, leaving Honey alone with the pony. Honey unfolded the travel sheet someone had left hanging neatly over a blanket bar and lowered it over the mare's luminous coat.

"Ready for this, girl?" she murmured as she buckled the front snaps. She smiled as she felt Minnie's nose dip down to nuzzle her hair. Straightening up, Honey slipped both arms around the pony's neck, not caring what Lani might say about staying clean. "We're going to have an amazing day," she whispered, barely loud enough to hear her own words. Minnie's ears pricked curiously. "No need to think about tomorrow, right? Not yet."

A few minutes later the grey mare was loaded into the three-horse trailer, which was hooked up to Ms Phillips' pick-up truck. Kelly was riding with her, while Honey and her friends were following behind with Ms Carmichael in her car. Honey had brought along the

CD she'd bought of the music she would be riding to that day. Dylan slipped it into the car's CD player and cranked up the volume.

"OK," she said briskly. "Just remember, Honey – be confident. That's half the battle."

Lani nodded. "Just pretend you're riding in a regular lesson," she suggested. "That way you won't worry so much about being perfect."

"Oh?" Ms Carmichael arched one eyebrow, glancing at her in the rear-view mirror.

Lani grinned and shrugged. "You know what I mean," she said. "Obviously we all want to be perfect in your lessons, too. But if we're not—"

"Nobody's there filming it," Dylan finished for her.

Malory was tapping her fingers along with the music. "Here's the part when you're supposed to do a walk to trot transition and then go right on to a spiral," she said. "Don't forget to keep Minnie bent a little going into it so she doesn't fall out on her shoulder."

Honey nodded. "Thanks, I will."

"And keep her moving forward," Lani put in. "You don't want her to peter out in the middle of the spiral or you'll lose the rhythm."

"Right," Dylan agreed. "Especially since you have to canter right after that."

Ms Carmichael burst out laughing. "You know, I might just have to retire and let you all take over my lessons!" she exclaimed with a twinkle in her eye. "But in the meantime, pipe down and let Honey focus. There's not much point playing her music if she can't even hear it over all your talking!"

"Wow, this place is huge!" Malory said, staring wide-eyed as Ms Carmichael pulled into a free parking spot outside the same fancy barn and indoor arena where Honey had auditioned before.

"Isn't it amazing?" Honey glanced around the parking lot. "Last time it was all filled with horse trailers out here, though."

"Yeah," Lani said. "I wonder what all these trucks and stuff are for?"

Dylan leaned forward for a better look, nearly bumping her nose on the dashboard as the truck stopped. "I've seen all kinds of location shoots for movies and TV shows back home in New York," she said. "They always have a bunch of trucks around. They're mostly for the equipment, I think – cameras, lighting, all that kind of stuff. Plus trailers for the stars, of course." She sat up, looking excited. "Hey, Honey, I wonder if you'll have your own trailer?"

"She does." Ms Carmichael cut the ignition and nodded at the Chestnut Hill horse trailer, which had pulled in just ahead of them. "That one. Come on, let's unload Minnie and get inside."

As they walked into the enormous indoor arena a few minutes later with pony in tow, a hyper-looking young woman with wild yellow hair came rushing over. "Are you Felicity Harper?" she barked at Malory.

"Nope. She is." Malory pointed at Honey.

"Fabulous. Come on, darling, we need to get you into make-up." The woman gestured for Honey to follow her.

Soon Honey was planted in a swivel chair in one of the trailers outside. *Seems Dylan was right after all*, she thought with amusement as several make-up artists clustered around her, patting powder and who knew what else on to her face. *I do have my own trailer – well, sort of!*

It was so much fun being treated like a superstar that she almost forgot to be nervous. Having her hair and make-up done professionally felt amazing. Honey couldn't believe the beautiful girl in the mirror was her! When they were finished, more people appeared and whisked her away to another trailer, where they dressed her in a gorgeous new outfit: spotless white breeches, butter-soft black leather riding boots, and a tailored black jacket that made her feel incredibly glamorous and grown-up.

When Honey stepped back into the indoor ring, her friends were waiting for her, watching as Ms Phillips lunged Minnie to help loosen her up after the trailer ride. Dylan's eyes widened when she took in Honey's new and improved appearance.

"Whoa," she exclaimed. "Are those Pikeur full-seats you're wearing?"

"I don't know." Honey glanced down at her pristine breeches. "They might be. I was told to put them on, so I did. Do they look all right?"

"Fab." Lani circled her, taking in the entire outfit.

"I like the jacket, too – very snazzy, and fits just right. Actually, it looks like the whole shebang was custom-made for you."

Malory nodded. "You look really nice, Honey."

Dylan shook her head admiringly. "These TV people don't mess around," she said. "I only wish Lynsey were here to see this. She'd die if she knew someone else had a fancier, more expensive riding outfit than hers!"

Just then Honey spotted Mr Hutton hurrying towards her with a smile on his face. "Hello, Honey," he greeted her. "You look great! Ready to do this?"

"I think so." Honey glanced anxiously towards Minnie, who was still trotting around on the lunge line. "Um, but Minnie's not quite ready yet. But if you give us five minutes, we can get her tacked up. . ."

The director chuckled. "No hurry. We're still setting up the equipment, so you have plenty of time. Just relax and help yourself to something from the catering trailer if you like."

"Catering trailer?" Dylan licked her lips. "Does that invitation apply to all of us?"

"I take it you're Miss Harper's entourage, eh?" Mr Hutton said with a smile.

"You bet!" Lani said. "She never goes anywhere without us."

"In that case, be my guests!"

By the time the girls returned from the catering trailer, Ms Carmichael, Kelly and Ms Phillips had Minnie tacked up in a gleaming black dressage saddle with a crisp white quilted pad. Her bridle was still hanging over Kelly's shoulder and a petite woman was hovering around near the mare's head.

"Who's that?" Dylan mumbled through a mouthful of doughnut.

"I'm not sure," Malory said. "But if I had to guess, I'd say it's Minnie's make-up person."

Sure enough, when the girls got closer, they could see that the woman was carefully applying liquid black make-up and baby oil around Minnie's eyes and nose to make them look even more striking against her snowy white coat. The make-up artist glanced up as the girls approached.

"Almost finished, Miss Harper," she said politely. "Sorry to keep you waiting."

"Er, no problem," Honey said. She could see Dylan and Lani exchanging a look and guessed that her friends were impressed by the way everyone was treating her.

"Did you girls get something to eat?" Ms Carmichael asked, switching Minnie's lead rope around so the make-up lady could do the other side of the mare's face. "I know we left school pretty early, and it's going to be a long day."

"They did," Honey said as her friends all nodded. "Lani wouldn't let me get near the food for fear of ruining my outfit."

"Hey, I said you could have a piece of dry toast if you wanted," Lani said. "But you said your stomach was too full of butterflies to eat anyway."

"True," Honey admitted. She shot a look over at all the camera equipment and lighting, which a bunch of crew members were busily moving around and adjusting. A shiver ran through her at the thought that soon, very soon, all that equipment would be pointed straight at her and Minnie. "Actually," she added with a gulp, "if you don't need me, I might duck outside for a bit of fresh air."

"Want me to come with you?" Lani asked.

Honey shook her head and smiled. "Thanks. But I'm all right on my own."

She headed for the door leading outside. The air had warmed up as the morning wore on, but there was still a cool breeze rustling through the new leaves of the trees lining the long drive. Honey tilted her head up and closed her eyes, enjoying the feel of the wind against her face. She opened her eyes again at the crunch of gravel nearby. A car had just turned up the drive and was heading towards the barn area. A high fieldstone wall blocked most of it from view at the moment, but Honey could see enough of the roof to guess that it was her father's saloon.

Her heart jumped into her throat. She'd been so busy, nervous and excited all morning that she'd forgotten about the move for the first time. Not wanting her mood to come crashing down now of all times, she turned and ducked back inside before her family could make it past the wall and spot her standing there.

"Got it?" Mr Hutton patted Honey kindly on the shoulder. "And don't worry, sweetheart. If you lose your

142

place, just stop and raise your hand and we'll start again. That's the magic of television."

The assistant director, a stout redheaded woman with a kind face, nodded. "The important thing here is the mood and feeling," she added. "We can do as many takes as we need to get the right movements."

"I see," Honey said. "Much different to being on stage where you only have one chance, I suppose!"

She smiled as the two adults chuckled. The director and his assistant had waylaid her as soon as she'd returned from her fresh-air break, wanting to give her final instructions. From where they were standing near the main cluster of cameras, Honey was vaguely aware that her parents and Sam had come in and were hovering around the rest of the Chestnut Hill gang, watching as Kelly and Malory finished getting Minnie tacked up.

"Come along, Miss Harper." One of the production assistants appeared, holding a gorgeous velvet helmet. "Your pony is waiting. Let's get you on board."

"OK." Honey took the helmet and settled it on her head. Like the rest of her outfit, it fitted perfectly.

She followed as the PA led her into the arena by the nearest of the two gates. Ms Carmichael had just led Minnie in through the other gate across the way. Honey glanced over and saw Dylan and Malory standing at the fence watching, while nearby her parents chatted with Ms Phillips. She had to crane her head to see her brother, who was a little way back with Lani.

"Ready, Honey?" Ms Carmichael asked as she and Minnie met Honey in the centre of the ring.

"As ready as I'll ever be, I suppose." Honey took a deep breath and reached out to give Minnie a pat, hoping her glove didn't leave any dust on the mare's spotless coat – or vice versa.

Ms Carmichael smiled. "Just relax and try to have fun. You're going to do fine." She turned to check Minnie's girth one last time, then slung the reins over the mare's head and turned to face Honey. "I'll give you a leg-up."

Honey's nerves steadied as soon as she settled into the saddle. Minnie felt warm and familiar beneath her as she stood waiting for her cue.

"Here we go, girl," Honey whispered as Ms Carmichael and the PA hurried back to the fence. "Almost time to dance."

She sent Minnie into a walk, aiming for the rail. Mr Hutton had told her to take a few minutes to warm-up and get familiar with the arena. When she was ready, she was supposed to halt in the centre of the arena to let the sound people know they could start the music.

Minnie felt loose and relaxed thanks to the earlier lungeing session. Honey was about to ask for a trot when she heard a commotion nearby. Turning her head, she saw Lani shoving her way past the people at the gate.

To her surprise, Lani came stomping right into the ring, leaving footprints in the carefully raked footing. Honey barely had time to wonder what was going on before her friend raced up to her, making Minnie halt abruptly to avoid running her over.

"Why didn't you tell me?" Lani hissed, her eyes flashing fire. "Sam just told me you're moving back to England!"

Honey gasped. Her face went hot, and her hands started to tremble as they clutched the reins.

Lani had tears in her eyes as she glared up at her. "So it's true?" she said. "I can't believe this. I thought we were friends!"

{ 13 }

"Lani, please!" Honey blurted out, her voice shaking. "We *are* friends – best friends. You know we are. I just didn't want to ruin things. I—"

"Please, miss!" A bearded man appeared and grabbed Lani by the arm. "We're about to start filming. You'll have to stay outside the ring."

Lani stared at Honey for a long moment, then turned, shook off the man's hand, and marched the rest of the way out of the ring, pushing past a confused-looking Dylan and Malory.

Honey felt terrible. All along she'd been thinking she was doing her friends a favour by keeping her terrible news a secret. But now she realized how it must seem to Lani to find out that her best friend had been lying to her for a full week – especially about something so important. How could she have been so selfish? She clenched her hands so tightly on the reins that Minnie shook her head in protest.

That brought Honey back to reality. She let the reins drop, flexing her fingers and taking a deep breath as she tried to regain control of her emotions.

Yes, I really messed up, she told herself. *But I'll have to deal with Lani – and the others – later. Because Minnie is one of my best friends, too, and I owe it to her to make the most of this amazing chance. Everyone deserves to see just how special she is.*

Taking another deep breath, she closed her eyes for a second. When she opened them, she felt a little calmer. Clucking softly to Minnie, she gathered up her reins again and rode to the centre of the arena. Then she glanced over at Mr Hutton and waited.

The lights dimmed, leaving only a pair of criss-crossing pale blue spotlights focused on girl and horse. A second later the music began, familiar after countless listens over the course of the past week. Everything else faded away as Honey let the melody flow through her.

This is it, girl, she thought. *Let's dance.*

Minnie sprang into an effortless trot, her neck arched and her mouth caressing the bit. And just like that, they were dancing. Honey forgot all about the cameras, the lights, the people watching from the shadowy, distant world outside the ring. All that existed for that moment was her and her amazing pony, who floated like a butterfly, her polished hooves barely seeming to touch the ground. Honey flowed with her as if they were one, hardly needing to twitch her leg or touch the reins to send Minnie into yet another graceful movement.

When the music ended, everyone watching burst into

147

applause. The spotlights shifted and Honey squinted over at Mr Hutton. He was smiling and giving her a thumbs up as he hurried into the ring.

"That was fantastic, Honey!" he said when he reached her. "You got it absolutely perfect on the first take. Are you sure you're not a pro?"

Honey smiled. "Pretty sure, yes," she said, giving Minnie a pat. "My pony's definitely a pro, though."

The director chuckled. "That's obvious," he agreed. "Anyway, we'd like to run through certain sections a few more times to get some different angles. All right?"

"Sure," Honey said. "Just tell me what you want me to do."

They spent the next half hour or so repeating various parts of the routine. Minnie responded just as well each time, and Mr Hutton seemed increasingly pleased.

"I think we've got it," he said at last as Honey stopped the mare by the fence. "This has to be one of the quickest and easiest shoots in the history of television, eh, guys?" He glanced at his crew with a grin.

One of the assistants nodded. "For sure," she agreed. "Especially for one with an animal involved. That's one nice pony."

Honey couldn't stop smiling as several others chimed in with more compliments about Minnie. She patted the mare proudly, feeling more privileged than ever for the chance to ride such an amazing pony.

"So that's it?" she asked, almost sorry to realize the shoot was over. "We're finished?"

"Yep," Mr Hutton said. "Thank you very much. Now take that little horse of yours and feed her some carrots, all right?"

"I will. Thanks."

Honey rode Minnie over to the gate, where Ms Carmichael was waiting with her halter. Honey's friends were gathered there, too, smiling and cheering – including Lani. Only someone who knew her as well as Honey did could ever have noticed that Lani's smile looked a bit strained as she pumped her fist and whooped loudly. It meant a lot to Honey to see her doing that even though she knew Lani still had to be terribly angry with her.

"Way to go, Harper!" Dylan shouted, racing up and giving Minnie a fond kiss on the neck. "You were awesome!"

Malory was grinning from ear to ear. "Who says horses can't dance? That was amazing!"

"Thanks, you guys." They had cleared the gate by now, so Honey kicked out of her stirrups and dismounted. As soon as her feet hit the ground, a wave of exhaustion rolled over her. She started to turn to run up her stirrups, but staggered and had to steady herself on Minnie's shoulder.

"Whoa," Dylan said, hurrying forward to catch her. "You OK?"

"Just tired, I guess," Honey said. "Concentrating so hard wore me out. Plus you guys wouldn't let me eat all day, remember?"

Malory had already sprung forward to take care of

the stirrups for her, so Honey took off her helmet and stuck it on the gatepost. Dylan turned away to scratch Minnie on the withers and coo over her, and Lani took the opportunity to lean closer to Honey.

"I didn't tell them yet," she murmured, not quite meeting Honey's eye.

Honey nodded. She'd already guessed that, but she felt a new wave of gratitude towards Lani. "Thanks," she whispered back.

Lani backed off as Ms Carmichael stepped towards them. "You were fantastic, Honey," the riding director said. "Now go rest while we take care of Minnie – you deserve it." She winked. "But don't expect this kind of star treatment to continue after today. You'll still be expected to untack your own pony after lessons just like everyone else."

Honey chuckled. "Thanks, Ms Carmichael." Then her gaze wandered past the riding director to where her parents and Sam were hovering uncertainly a few metres beyond.

As soon as she saw them, she found herself almost overwhelmed with love and joy. Even though she'd acted as if she didn't care whether they came to watch the shoot or not, she knew it wouldn't have been the same without having them there. This was her moment, and she wanted to share it with the people who mattered most.

She ran over and found herself enveloped in a big group hug. "Thanks for coming," she mumbled into her father's lapel.

"Oh, Honey," her mother exclaimed. "You were just wonderful! We're so proud."

Honey pulled back and gazed at them. "I'm really glad you're here," she said. "I wouldn't have blamed you for staying away considering how badly I've acted this week."

"Of course we came," Mr Harper said, slinging one arm over her shoulders and giving her another squeeze. "People in families argue all the time. But that doesn't mean we shouldn't be there for one another when it matters."

"Yeah." Sam rolled his eyes. "Don't be such a drama queen, sis. Oh, I forgot." He shot a look towards the cameras. "You *are* a drama queen now, aren't you?"

Honey couldn't help laughing. Her brother had always been able to cheer her up with his goofy sense of humour.

Just then a man hurried towards them. Honey had vaguely noticed him watching earlier – he was difficult to miss, with his expensive Italian suit, funky green sunglasses perched atop his slicked-back hair, and cool leather jacket slung over one shoulder.

"Sorry to interrupt," the man said. "I just wanted to come over and say hello and congratulations to the young lady." He smiled at Honey. "My name is Tim Hedges and I'm a talent agent."

"Hello," Mr Harper said, shaking the man's hand. He quickly introduced himself and his wife. "Lovely to meet you, Mr Hedges."

"Call me Tim," the agent said. Then he turned his

attention back to Honey. "Miss Harper, you're what I like to call a natural star."

"I am?" Honey said.

"She is?" Sam shot her a look.

The man nodded, once more addressing Honey's parents. "I believe there could be a lot of work in your daughter's future if she cares to pursue it," he told them. "Modelling, more commercials, maybe even some acting in films or TV. I'd love to talk to you about the possibility of my agency representing her and helping shape her career." He reached into his pocket. "Here's my card if you'd like to set up a meeting."

Mr Harper accepted the business card, looking surprised. "Oh, I see," he said. "We'll have to discuss it further and get back to you."

"Terrific. I hope to see you again soon, Miss Harper," the agent said.

"Er, you can call me Honey," Honey replied, not sure how else to respond to all this.

"Honey?" Mr Hedges looked surprised. "I thought your name was Felicity."

"That's her real name," Sam put in. "But everyone calls her Honey. She likes to pretend it's after her honey-coloured hair, but really it's because she was fascinated with bees when we were little and kept catching them by hand, though somehow she never got stung."

The agent looked delighted. "Honey Harper," he murmured. "It's the perfect stage name!"

After he said goodbye and left, Honey glanced at her parents. "Why'd you say we'll talk about it?" she asked quietly. "I'm not even going to be in the States much longer."

Her parents exchanged a glance. "We've been discussing that, actually," her father said.

Mrs Harper nodded. "We realize there's little point forcing you to move back if you're truly happier here," she said. "Since you board anyway, it's not much different you being here or at your old school back home."

"And you can still fly home for school breaks and holidays," her father added.

Honey gasped. "Really? I can stay at Chestnut Hill?" she cried. Then she noticed her brother standing there watching her, looking uncharacteristically solemn. "But what about Sam?" she added, dismay stabbing through her at the thought of being a whole ocean's width away from her twin. "He can stay too, can't he? He could board at St Kit's instead of commuting – I know it's the middle of term, but I'm sure if you talked to the school to see if there's enough space. . ."

Her words trailed off as she saw both her parents shaking their heads. "I'm afraid not," her father said with a sigh. "Sam's still in remission. We couldn't let him be so far away just now."

"Yeah." Sam shrugged. "But that's OK. I can still harass you via email, sis."

Honey forced a smile. She'd known as soon as she asked the question what the answer would be. Still, it broke her heart to think of being so far away from her brother.

Her mother stepped forward and gave her a hug. "In any case, we'll leave the decision up to you," she said. "Think it over and let us know what you'd like to do, all right? In the meantime, just know that we're terribly proud of you."

"Thanks, Mum." Honey hugged her back hard. Her head was spinning with the possibility of staying at Chestnut Hill after all. But right now, she was happy just to be here with her mother's arms wrapped around her, making her feel safe and loved.

"Miss Harper! Miss Harper! Over here!" Jennifer Quinn and Tessa Harding dashed forward, sliding towards Honey on their knees and snapping away with their digital cameras as they pretended to be pushy paparazzi.

Honey giggled as she climbed out of Ms Carmichael's car. They'd just pulled into the stable yard at Chestnut Hill after the shoot. Tons of people had gathered to greet them. Honey even spotted several of her Adams House dorm-mates who rarely ventured anywhere near the stable yard, like Razina and Faith from the Get Crafty club. She was even more surprised when Lynsey and Patience nudged their way to the front of the crowd. They were dressed in outfits that looked better suited to a weekend in New York: fake fur jackets, indigo skinny jeans and knee-high Gucci-style boots. Honey wondered if they thought she might have brought some talent spotters back with her in the horse truck.

The chilly start to the morning had mellowed into a

gorgeous afternoon hinting at the spring weather yet to come. The sun gleamed down on the fresh grass poking up in the pastures and the leaves unfurling in the trees, making the rolling hills surrounding the stables almost impossibly beautiful. Honey glanced out at one of the paddocks that lay beyond the riding rings just in time to see Quest and another gelding named Soda rear up on their hind legs, flail playfully at each other, and then take off bucking and snorting across the paddock together. She smiled, though for a second she was afraid she might burst into tears at the sheer loveliness of it all.

I'm so lucky to have all this, she thought, her gaze shifting to her friends.

Dylan had already waded out into the crowd of well-wishers. She was eagerly describing the day's adventure to anyone who cared to listen, using plenty of hand gestures – and, if Honey guessed right, a bit of exaggeration. Malory had hurried over to the horse trailer and was helping Kelly and Ms Carmichael unload Minnie. Lani was busy convincing a couple of bystanders how much fun it would be to help carry the tack and other equipment into the barn and put it away.

Yes, Honey thought, blinking away another threat of tears. Her hand strayed up to her throat, touching the horse pendant Josh had given her, which she'd worn all day under her riding clothes. *I really am the luckiest girl in the world*.

"I still can't believe they let you keep this outfit." Dylan rubbed the fabric of the gorgeous black dressage jacket between her fingers one last time before hanging it up in Honey's closet. "Lynsey's going to have a cow when she sees it."

"It was awfully nice of them," Honey agreed as she tucked her new dress boots into the closet as well. "Though these clothes are so posh it's going to be a bit scary to wear them anywhere near a horse."

Malory laughed from her position perched on the edge of Lani's desk. "Yeah. Horses don't care if your breeches cost a dollar at the thrift store or a million bucks from some fancy catalogue. They'll happily snort green slime all over them either way."

When Honey turned away from the closet, she saw Lani sitting cross-legged on her bed staring at her. Honey nodded, knowing it was time to come clean.

"Listen," she said. "I have something I need to talk to you about."

"What is it?" Dylan wandered over and flopped on to Honey's bed, reaching for the issue of *Practical Horseman* lying on the nightstand. "Are you about to tell us you're moving?"

"What?" Honey blurted out, shooting a look towards Lani, who looked equally surprised. "But how did you know I— Who— Did Sam tell you, too?"

"Huh?" Dylan looked up from the magazine and blinked. "Did Sam tell me what? I was just going to say that you'll probably be jetting off to Hollywood now that you've. . . Hang on a second." She tossed aside the magazine and sat up. "What are we talking about here?"

Malory looked alarmed, too. "Yeah, you look way too serious, Honey. What's up?"

"Just a moment." Honey held up both hands. "Let me start from the beginning." She shot another look at Lani, who nodded encouragingly. "See, it's like this. My dad has a new job in the UK beginning in May."

"What?" Dylan cried. "You mean *this* May?"

Malory was so startled that she slid down from the desk and almost tripped over a stack of books sitting beside it. "No!" she exclaimed.

Dylan shook her head vigorously. "We've got to stop this!" she declared, sounding on the verge of hysteria. "You can't leave us, Honey. No way! This place wouldn't be the same without you!"

"Wait," Lani ordered her. "She's not finished."

Honey smiled gratefully at her. She and Lani hadn't had much opportunity to talk privately. But she could tell by a few things she'd said that Sam must have filled her in on the revised situation before leaving the shoot.

"Right," Honey said. "The thing is, my parents are leaving it up to me what to do. I can either move back with them and go to school there, or stay here at Chestnut Hill and just fly to England for holidays."

"Oh my gosh!" Dylan collapsed on to her back on the bed, fanning herself with one hand. "Thank goodness! You should've just said that at the beginning – you practically gave me a heart attack!"

Malory laughed, sounding relieved. "Me too," she agreed. Then she hurried over to give Honey a hug. "I'm sure it'll be hard being so far away from your family, but we'll be right here for you, every single day."

"Too right!" Dylan jumped up and rushed over to join in the hug. "Don't worry, Honey. We'll keep you so busy you won't even have a chance to miss them!"

"Hey." Lani hurried towards them, stretching out her arms. "Make room for me!"

Honey just smiled and hugged them all back, though she also felt her heart sinking. As usual, Dylan hadn't even paused before reacting to what she thought Honey was telling her – namely, that she would definitely be staying at Chestnut Hill – and the others seemed perfectly willing to follow along. How could Honey correct them now?

They seem to believe this is an easy decision for me, she thought. *A no-brainer, as Dylan would say. How can I tell them that I haven't made up my mind yet? That I still need some time to think it over before I choose?*

As the hug fell apart, Honey opened her mouth to say something. But Dylan and Malory were already chattering about getting hold of some of the pictures people had taken of Honey's homecoming down at the barn so they could add them to the collage. Lani had sat down at her desk and was staring at a baseball cap pinned up on her bulletin board. Honey wondered if she was thinking about Sam.

It'll be hard for her to lose him, she thought with a flash of sympathy for her friend. *Almost as hard as it would be for me to lose all of them. . .*

She let her mouth fall shut. After all, if she did decide

158

to stay, there was no point in making them worry again. And if she didn't? Well, she would just have to deal with that when the time came.

That night Honey awoke feeling as if she were flying, and realized she'd been dreaming about riding Minnie. She smiled, staring up at the dark ceiling.

Then she remembered the decision she still had to make, and her smile faded, replaced by a gnawing feeling in the pit of her stomach. Knowing she wouldn't be able to fall asleep again, she sat up and glanced over at the other bed. Lani was sleeping with her face towards the wall, snoring softly.

Moving slowly so she wouldn't wake her, Honey got out of bed and reached for her paddock boots, pulling them on over the socks she'd worn to bed. Then she tiptoed to the door and grabbed her jacket off the hook, shrugging it on over her flannel pyjamas before letting herself out of the room.

It was a brilliant moonlit night with just the merest hint of frost, reminding her that winter wasn't quite gone yet. Shoving her hands into her pockets for warmth, Honey hurried down the path towards the stable yard. Soon she was letting herself into the barn. Soft whickers greeted her from up and down the aisle, and Morello gave his door a sharp kick as he whinnied for attention. But Honey paused only long enough to pat the feisty skewbald pony on his nose before continuing down the aisle to Minnie's stall.

The pretty grey mare had her head out over the

half-door, her delicate ears pricked. She let out a snuffle as Honey let herself into the stall and wrapped her arms around the pony's neck.

"Oh, Minnie," Honey breathed. "You're the best pony in the whole entire world. Did I ever tell you that?"

Minnie bent her neck and lipped at the pocket of Honey's jacket. Realizing she probably had some stray treats in there, Honey fished into the pocket until she came up with a handful of carrot pieces. She held them out so Minnie could pluck them delicately from her hand.

"Well, it's true," she said as the mare crunched down on the treats. "You are. And I didn't need a TV commercial to figure it out." Her eyes filled with tears as she leaned forward to hug the pony again. "Because you make me feel like a superstar every time I ride you."

{ 14 }

"Rise and shine!" Lani sang out, yanking the duvet off Honey. "Even superstars have to get up for breakfast eventually, you know."

Honey let out a groan. By the time she'd returned from the yard the night before, she was worn out. She'd fallen straight back to sleep, but now it felt as if she'd barely closed her eyes at all.

"Hurry up and get dressed." Lani dropped the duvet on the floor, then hurried across the room to the closet. "We're supposed to be meeting Dylan and Mal for brunch in less than ten minutes. And you know how cranky Dylan gets when she's hungry."

"All right, all right." Honey yawned and sat up, feeling more alert already at the thought of brunch. There were few things tastier in the world than the Chestnut Hill cafeteria's special banana-nut pancakes. "I'll be ready in a jiffy."

The pancakes were as delicious as ever, and a fresh mango smoothie chased away any lingering weariness. Honey and the others spent most of the meal discussing the shoot, the collage, and various other subjects, though the topic of the move never came up.

"We'd better get going," Malory said at last, checking her watch. "I signed us up for a trail ride today, and we don't want someone else to come along and steal our favourite ponies out from under us if we're late."

"Not much chance of that, at least for you, Mal." Dylan gulped down the last of her orange juice. "Nobody else in her right mind would want to ride Tyb, especially out on the trails on a brisk spring morning when he had the entire day before off!"

Malory stuck out her tongue, pretending to be insulted. Lani laughed.

"She's got you there, Mal," she agreed. "And I guess Honey doesn't have to worry, either. She's the only one allowed to ride Minnie without Dylan's say so."

"I guess that leaves you and me, Hernandez," Dylan quipped. "We'd better get down there so we don't end up riding Blaze and Bella."

Honey couldn't help smiling at the thought of her two lively friends yawning their way through a sedate walk in the woods on two of Chestnut Hill's slowest, laziest ponies. Still, she knew Dylan was mostly joking. Ms Carmichael would never let anyone steal any of their ponies if she knew they were coming.

Soon Honey, Lani, Malory and Dylan were trotting along a twisting, sun-dappled trail through the woods. All four of the ponies had started out alert and ready to go, though Minnie had soon settled into her usual calm demeanour and Colorado was being uncharacteristically

162

lazy, probably due to the warm day and his fast-growing coat, which hadn't been clipped lately since he hadn't been in the last show.

"Chill out, Morello!" Dylan exclaimed, sitting deep in her saddle and half halting as her pony, who was in the lead at the moment, snorted and tried to surge forward as they rounded a bend in the trail.

"He's pretty full of beans today, huh?" Malory puffed, sitting tight as Tybalt spooked at a passing bird and skittered to one side. "Tyb is, too. I think we'd better let them canter soon and get some energy out."

"Sounds good to me," Dylan agreed. "Should we let them go when we get to that next meadow? It's a nice big flat one with no groundhog holes that I know of."

"You guys go ahead," Lani spoke up. "I don't want Colorado to get too sweaty, and he's not really in the mood anyway. Maybe Honey and I can meet up with you at the folly, OK?"

Dylan looked surprised as she glanced back over her shoulder, but she just shrugged. "Suit yourself," she said. "Come on, Mal. We're almost there. You ready?"

"Yup," Malory replied, already nudging Tybalt forward.

A moment later the two of them reached a broad, sunny meadow dotted with early spring wild flowers. "And they're off!" Dylan shouted in a pretty good imitation of a racetrack announcer as she released Morello and he rocketed forward into a full gallop with Tybalt hot on his tail.

Colorado's head flew up and he danced in place, snorting as he watched the other ponies race off. "Sure you don't want to go with them?" Honey asked Lani. "I know Minnie and I can't come close to keeping up with the rest of you, but I'm sure we could manage a nice canter."

Lani half halted firmly, turning Colorado down a side trail to distract him. As soon as the others were out of his sight, the gelding's head drooped and he seemed content to amble along, enjoying the sultry weather.

"I don't mind," Lani said, giving her pony a pat. "Let's go this way. It's a shortcut to the folly."

A few minutes later they were fording the stream and heading up the hill towards the folly, a pretty stone tower that had been built as a picturesque ruin by a previous owner of the property. It was one of Honey's favourite spots on campus, partly because it reminded her of the ancient stone cottages near her English home.

The two friends dismounted in the dappled clearing right outside the folly. As Minnie and Colorado ducked their heads to nibble at some spring greens peeking through the matted leaves, Lani turned to face Honey with a serious look on her face.

"Listen, Honey," she said. "I just wanted to talk to you about yesterday."

Honey bit her lip. "Me too," she said. "I'm really sorry I didn't tell you myself. It's just—"

"Wait," Lani interrupted before she could finish, playing with Colorado's reins, which she was holding in one hand while the pony grazed. "It's OK. I understand. I just sort of flew off the handle at first 'cause I hadn't stopped to think about it, you know?" She shrugged sheepishly. "I do that sometimes."

"I know." Honey smiled. "But I really am sorry."

Lani nodded. "You can talk to me about anything, you know," she said. "We'll always be friends – best friends. No amount of distance could ever change that."

Honey stared at her wordlessly. Maybe Dylan and Malory assumed the decision was already over and done with, but now she realized that Lani knew her better than that. She'd guessed that Honey hadn't yet made up her mind about whether to return to the UK or stay at Chestnut Hill.

Emotions bubbled up inside her, but she knew she'd never be able to put them into words. Instead she reached over and took Lani's free hand in her own.

"Thanks," she whispered.

"Yum!" Dylan declared, licking icing off her fingers. "If this is what we have to look forward to in ninth grade life sciences, I can't wait!"

Tanisha Appleton laughed. She and the rest of the Adams freshmen had invited the rest of the dorm into the common room to sample a devil's food cake they'd made to practise for cooking class. "We can't take all the credit," Tanisha said. "Who knows what would have happened if Mrs Herson hadn't noticed we almost forgot to add the baking powder?"

Honey reached for another piece of cake. She hadn't eaten much the day before, and despite doing her best to make up for it at brunch, she'd worked up quite an appetite on that trail ride. She was just finishing the second piece when the door swung open and Ms Carmichael hurried in. Dylan spotted her, too.

"Hey, Aunt Ali, er, Ms Carmichael, er. . ." she said. "Are you here because you want to take your beloved niece and her friends out for a fancy dinner tonight, or are you here to yell at your favourite riding student because she might have possibly forgotten to hang up her bridle after her trail ride today?"

"Neither, actually." Ms Carmichael chuckled and held up the laptop she was carrying. "I'm here to see Honey. Jim Hutton just emailed me the early rushes of the TV commercial, and I thought she'd like to take a look."

"Oh, wow!" Honey's heart jumped. "Really? I'd love to!"

Soon she and her friends were gathered around the laptop, along with everyone else who happened to be in the common room. Ms Carmichael tapped a few keys to get things started, then stepped back out of the way.

The screen went dark for a second. Then some technical information flashed up, mostly about the advertising agency, as far as Honey could tell. That faded away as well, and then a girl on a white pony filled the screen. Music swelled in the background.

"Check it out!" Razina whispered, sounding amazed. "Is that really you, Honey?"

Honey could hardly believe it herself. She was stunned by how polished she looked in her fancy dressage outfit. And Minnie was positively waltzing around the ring, looking as light as a butterfly!

When the footage finished, the room erupted in cheers. "That was awesome!" Alexandra cried.

"Yeah," Aggninder Dillon put in. "Now we can all say we knew you before you were famous, Honey!"

"Speech! Speech!" Dylan shouted, pounding on the coffee table.

Honey tried to refuse, but others joined in. "Come on, Honey," Rosie Williams said with a wink. "Just say a few words for your fans."

"You're going to have to get used to it, you know," Dylan added. "TV stars have to give lots of interviews and stuff all the time."

Lani poked Honey in the side. "Go on," she said with a smile. "Everyone's waiting."

Honey climbed to her feet and looked at the upturned, smiling faces surrounding her. All those familiar faces – the people she'd gotten to know since coming to Chestnut Hill as a scared seventh-grader the previous autumn.

She took a deep breath. "Thank you for being so amazing," she began. "All of you." She glanced from her friends and dorm-mates over to Ms Carmichael, who was smiling at her. "Before I came to Chestnut Hill, I'd never have been able to do anything like that. Or been able to ride a pony like Minnie – special thanks for that one, Dylan."

Dylan grinned. "Thank you, thank you," she said, taking a mini bow in her seat.

Next Honey turned to face Malory. "Special thanks to you, Mal, as well," she went on. "You've really been an inspiration in my riding, plus you always seem to know what everyone else is feeling, even me." As Malory blushed, Honey looked over to Lani. "And of course I want to thank Lani for, well, just being the best friend and room-mate ever. I truly can't believe my luck that I've met all of you. You've given me a million chances to do amazing things, and I'll never forget any of them."

She paused, not sure what else she wanted to say. But then, all of a sudden, she knew. In fact, she was pretty sure she'd known it all along – she just hadn't been sure she'd have the courage. So she plunged on ahead before she could lose her nerve.

"Anyway, since you all mean so much to me, I wanted you all to know something," she said. "I have some big news. My family is moving back to the UK soon. And I—" She took one last deep breath. "I'll be going with them."

Look out for the final book
in the *Chestnut Hill* series!

Lauren Brooke

Chestnut
Hill

Far and Away

Have you read the first books in the *Chestnut Hill* series?